WORTH THE FIGHT

THE RISKS WE TAKE DUET 2

BELLA MATTHEWS

Copy Editor: Dena Mastrogiovanni, Red Pen Editing

Cover Designer: Shannon Passmore, Shanoff Designs

Photographer: Wander Aguiar, Wander Aguiar Photography

Formatting: Savannah Richey, Peachy Keen Author Services

Heather ~ I don't know that I would have ever made it to the end of this book without you. Thank you for every note. Every laugh. Every message. Sometimes people come into our lives, and we feel the difference right away. Thank you for being that person.

"There will be dozens of people who will take your breath away, but the one who reminds you to breathe is the one you should keep."

— UNKNOWN

SENSITIVE CONTENT

This book contains sensitive content that could be triggering.

Please see my website for a full list.
WWW.AUTHORBELLAMATTHEWS.COM

COOPER

NOBODY WARNED ME WHAT IT'S LIKE TO LOOK BACK WITH regret.

To be left wondering, *What if . . . ?*

What if I'd told her sooner?

What if I hadn't missed the signs?

It was my job to protect them . . . What if I hadn't failed?

What if I'd only had a little more time?

COOPER

THE UNITED STATES GOVERNMENT DOESN'T NEGOTIATE with terrorists.

That's their official stance. But when those terrorists kidnap US citizens—who happen to also be the very beautiful daughter of a US ambassador and her best friend, who's the equally beautiful daughter of a very high-ranking FBI official, both overseas and volunteering for a peace mission—the official stance may be that we don't negotiate with terrorists. But the reality is they send us in to do it for them because the PR nightmare of letting these women be taken and tortured or sold would be worse.

Axe and I have been sitting for hours on top of this empty house in the hills of Pakistan, just outside of an old, abandoned village, waiting for the exchange to happen about one hundred yards west of us. "Dude. What the hell's wrong with you?" I adjust my scope and do a cursory look around, zeroing in on Ford and Linc, who are waiting outside of the first vehicle, with Trick and Rook in the second one. "You haven't stopped fidgeting."

Axel grabs a protein bar from his bag and throws half of it my way. "They're thirty fucking minutes late. I've got a bad feeling about this." He chews his bar, then looks back out at the designated meeting zone. "Why the hell is Linc with Ford anyway? It should be Rook and Ford."

"Ford wanted Linc today." I don't give anymore thought

to it than that. He's the team leader, and he makes those calls.

Through my scope, I clock movement to the east, and speak into my coms, "Get your shit together and your party hats on, boys, because the guests just showed up."

A caravan of old military vehicles is heading down the winding dirt road toward our team, who waits to make the handoff.

I make my adjustments and settle in, while Command gives information through our coms.

Axel hunkers down in place on the other end of the roof and prepares to have the team's back, should anything go wrong.

The fucking dirt kicks up with the dry wind that's always present in this sand pit as two men emerge from the first vehicle, followed by two more from the second. All of them carry AK-47s strapped around their necks.

The men from the second vehicle pull two hooded women from the car and shove them out in front of them, digging the barrels of their guns into the women's backs. But they don't move toward Ford and Linc, leaving that instead to the other two men.

Ford holds the duffle full of money at his side but tells them he needs proof of life before he shows them the money.

"Remove the bags from their heads," Ford's voice filters through my earpiece.

"That's five million dollars in Ford's hands, Sinclair." Axe places his eye against his scope. "You ever seen five mill in cash before?"

"Nope. And we're not going to today either." Not from up here. "Get your fucking head in the game."

The potato sacks are ripped off both women, and yup, they're the women we're looking for. Banged up and

4

bruised, but they appear to be in one piece. "Confirmed," I say into my coms. "I have eyes on Saylor Reynolds and Calista Gallo."

Ford gives the signal to confirm he heard me.

"Shit." The guy from the first car turns, yelling something behind him. "What the fuck is he saying?" I ask anyone who can confirm.

"No clue," Rook answers into the coms. "He's too far away."

"He's moving. He's moving," Linc adds as the men behind the girls pull them back.

"Fuck. Something's got them spooked." I look into the hills but don't see anything.

"Disable the last car" is ordered. And I don't hesitate before taking out their tires.

"Are we taking out the others?" I ask, then look over at Axel, who's been strangely quiet. "Axe, man. You with me?"

He adjusts his body to line up better with his gun.

Ford doesn't answer as he tries to calm everyone down on the road. Both our team and theirs point guns at each other.

Fingers on the triggers.

One of their guys grabs the women.

And then, the world explodes.

There's a certain rhythm to a hospital room. It's in the hum of the lights. The buzzing of the machines. The movement of the staff. Like everything moves in perfect synch.

In my few short years in the Navy, I've woken up this way a time or two . . . maybe three. The difference this time is that I don't remember why.

When I force my dry eyes to open, the dark room takes a minute to come into focus, and even then, it's not crisp. What the fuck is wrong with my vision?

I attempt to sit up and immediately regret it as pain spikes up my abdomen, and a massive pressure in my head threatens to detonate.

"Relax, Sinclair." Ford's voice comes from my left—I think—and I turn my head slowly his way as a wave of nausea rolls through me. "I'll get the doc." A chair scrapes against the floor, and I groan in response to the offending noise.

"What happened?" I rasp quietly as I try to focus on Ford, who grabs something that looks like a crutch next to his chair and leans his weight on it to maneuver himself to the door of my room.

Why is everything out of focus?

Ford opens the door and speaks to someone on the other side, then makes his way back to me. "What *didn't* happen would be a better question," he groans as he slowly lowers himself down into the chair as the curtain between my bed and the one next to me opens.

Rook drops down into a chair next to Trick with a grunt.

Trick is lying in the other bed, with his leg casted from hip to toe and hanging from a metal thing above the bed. "The mission went FUBAR in a way none of us could have possibly expected."

I close my eyes and try to focus on something scratching at the back of my mind, but it doesn't come. I will myself to remember what happened, but I'm coming up blank. The room goes in and out of focus as my eyes attempt to adjust. "What the fuck?" I rub my eyes, trying to clear them. "What happened out there? Did we save the girls?"

The girls . . . We were there to save two women.

I think.

"What's the last thing you remember?" Ford adjusts his position at the foot of my bed.

"The last thing I remember was the team sitting in the command room, going over how to execute the mission." The pain behind my eyes settles to a dull ache as I try to focus on Ford but can't.

Rook leans his elbows on his knees. Dark circles surround his eyes, and a white bandage wrapped around his forearm pulls tight against his skin. "How're you feeling, Sinclair?"

"Like someone put my brain in a blender. Will one of you tell me what the fuck happened? Where are the other guys?" I don't dare try to move again, for fear of the pain in my head coming back.

Ford clears his throat. He and Rook are both in sweats, unlike Trick and me, who lie in our beds in hospital gowns.

"Where's Linc and Axe?"

Just then, a nurse in blue scrubs walks through my door and starts fussing with my chart. "How's your pain on a scale of one to ten, Petty Officer?"

"A two," I tell her without thinking it through, just wanting her out of the room so I can fill in the blanks.

"Now is not the time to be a hero, sailor. Your body will heal faster if it's not in as much pain." She checks the machine next to me, then she adjusts the starched white blanket around my waist and lifts my gown to check the bandage on my abdomen.

"Holy fuck. Was I shot?" I ignore the groan coming from Trick while I look down at my bandaged abdomen in shock.

"Yes. They had to go in and retrieve the bullet." She writes something in her chart, then rolls a tray my way and fills a cup with water. "A doctor will be with you shortly. Let me know if you need anything." She hands me the remote for the bed, then turns to Rook and Ford. "You're both supposed to be in your own rooms."

Ford smiles at her. "But you're not going to kick us out, are you, Denise?"

Denise shakes her head as she rolls her eyes and goes through a similar assessment with Trick before glaring back at Rook and Ford. "Leave the lights off and the blinds drawn for now. And no loud voices or noises or you both go back to your room. Got it?"

Both men agree before she shuts the door. Then they turn back to Trick and me without saying another word.

I push the button on the bed and adjust myself slowly to a sitting position, feeling the slight twinge in my side.

Damn. These must be some good meds.

"What the hell's going on? How long have I been out?" I demand.

Trick tries to adjust himself and winces. "Two days, brother. We both got out of surgery yesterday, but this is the first time you've woken up."

Rook leans back against the cabinet and groans, then looks at Ford while my brain tries to catch up. "What aren't you saying?"

"Linc's dead." Ford lifts his eyes to the ceiling. "The damn building came down on all of us." Ford blows out a long breath before adding, "We got one of the girls, but they still have the other."

"What?" There's a whooshing in my ears as I try to absorb what he just said.

He's not right.

He can't be fucking right.

"Linc—" The rest of the words stick in my throat.

He was my battle buddy all through boot camp.

We got each other through hell week together.

I don't want to believe they're right.

I can't.

Rook presses the palms of his hands against his face and rubs his eyes. "Yeah, man. Linc's gone . . . And it gets worse."

"What the fuck's worse than Linc being dead?" There's no way it can get worse.

Fury settles in Rook's face like I've never seen before. "Axe betrayed us."

"What?" Clearly, my brain isn't working at top speed, so there's no way I heard him right. "What the fuck did you just say?" My stomach drops as my blood roars.

Ford stands up, leaning against his crutch, and moves next to my bed. "Axel shot Linc. From what we've gathered, he was working with the terrorists."

I sit in stunned silence as Ford's words bounce around in my broken brain, like a puck trying to find the net in the air-hockey game Nat and I used to play when we were kids.

And why can I remember that, but not what happened? Wait. "Does anyone have any idea where Axe is?" I try to focus on Ford, but he's too far away, and my head throbs again in a brutal revolt.

A look passes between Ford and Rook that makes me brace for what's coming next because it's not going to be good. Even broken, that much is obvious to me. "Say it."

With a heavy sigh, Rook sits in the chair by my bed and seems to brace himself for whatever he's about to say. "Look, what I'm about to tell you doesn't leave this room."

"It doesn't look like I'm going anywhere anytime soon, brother." I motion to my body sitting under the starched hospital sheets.

Trick nods his agreement, and Ford, who already seems

to know what's about to be said, makes himself more comfortable against the door, crossing his ankles, and blocking anyone's entrance from interrupting us.

Rook exhales and leans forward, his forearms braced on his knees. "I've told you I have four brothers, right?" The corner of his mouth kicks up as his gaze sweeps the room. "I mean, other than you assholes."

Trick scoffs. "You fucking love us."

"Mm-hmm," he agrees, shaking his head.

"Yeah, you've mentioned them," I say, trying to keep us on track. My brain's having a hard enough time focusing. I don't need the extras right now.

"Okay, what you *don't* know is the five of us also have a half-brother."

I shrug. "And? So do I. That's not so unusual."

Rook grimaces. "My brothers and I all have the same father. Jasper Woods."

Trick frowns. "Why does that name sound familiar?"

"Because he runs Black Box Ops," Ford speaks up, the muscles in his jaw twitching. "He's also a decorated general. Retired a few years back and started his company. He hires ex-military contractors."

"Shit, I've heard of them." Most military men have. They're a mercenary company that works for the highest bidder, in both the government and private sector. They've been involved in some shady shit in the Middle East and Asia. They tend to recruit from branches of the military, focusing on the best of the best from each branch.

Rook sighs. "Jasper is a fucking maniac."

"We've all got family issues, man." Trick tries to play it off.

"Did your father murder your little brother?" Rook stares off to the side.

My heart slams in my chest. Fucking hell.

"Didn't think so," Rook says when no one speaks. "Jasper's involved in a lot of shit with a lot of guys."

"Like?" Trick presses.

"It's too much to get into, but my brother Court and some friends started Phoenix International. It's an organization that fights back against what Black Box does. They work in direct opposition to them. You guys know this is my last tour with the SEALs. I'm going to work for them when my contract's up."

My head pounds in time with my pulse. "What exactly are you saying?"

"Phoenix operates under the radar, but one of the guys Court is friends with is doing some digging into this op. So far? He's found quite a bit about the shit Axe has been up to. He made some deals with some nasty motherfuckers." Rook looks like he's swallowing nails.

"Who?" I grit out, wanting the details on why a guy I trusted with my life betrayed us and killed Linc.

"We're working on it," Rook mutters.

"There's a reason we're having this conversation now," Ford adds. "The mission we were on wasn't officially sanctioned. The Navy is going to minimize public and political fallout by burying as much shit as they can."

"Having a SEAL go AWOL probably doesn't look good for Uncle Sam," Trick snaps.

"Which is why I have my people looking into Axe," Rook states, his tone cold. "Axel was one of us. He betrayed *us*. I want fucking answers before we turn him over to the authorities. As soon as we find him, we'll handle this together."

"Hooyah, motherfuckers," Trick agrees with a savage grin.

Ford looks from Trick to me. "You two listen to the doctors and heal up. We'll need you soon enough."

I nod, frustrated that I'm stuck in this bed when I should be out there trying to find Axe.

I look at my friends—my brothers—and know I need to be there when this shit goes down.

There's no other option.

Whatever it takes, Axe has to answer for what he's done.

He's got to answer for Linc.

COOPER

A KNOCK ON THE DOOR LATER IN THE DAY PULLS ME FROM the thoughts running rampant in my sedated brain. A doctor glances at me and moves to pull the curtain between Trick and me closed. He stands next to my bed with a tablet in his hand. "Petty Officer Sinclair, I'm Dr. Bennett. I was the general surgeon on call when you came in."

"When can I get back in the field, Doc?" I know my abdomen will likely take a few weeks to heal, but I don't have a few weeks to wait around.

Dr. Bennett's dark eyes give away what he's thinking before he says it, and it's not going to be good. "We're going to need to talk about that . . ."

"Doc, my brain is kinda fuzzy right now. I must have heard you wrong. Can you say that again? What's there to talk about? Just give me a date." Then I begrudgingly add, "Maybe a little slower." If I didn't think it would split my skull in two, I'd try to shake the fog free from my head, but I don't think my brain can handle the movement yet.

"All concussions are considered TBI's. Traumatic brain injuries. You suffered a grade 3 concussion. I've brought in a neuro consult, and we've got reason to be concerned. You're scheduled to have another MRI later today. We'll know more after that. Until then, I can't give you any kind of estimate about if *or* when you'll be able to return to duty."

I want to argue with him that I'll be returning to my team, but my eyes grow heavy from the pain meds.

He checks something on the machine next to me, then steps back. "No lights, no electronics, and no excitement for the next twenty-four hours. Give yourself time to heal, Sinclair. We'll know more soon." He turns on his heel and leaves the same quiet way he came in, while I'm left trying to focus on the door he just walked through and the one word I can't shake.

If.

He said *if* or when I return to active duty.

He's wrong.

I'm a goddamn US Navy SEAL. I will return to duty. To my team.

I have to. It's who I am. It's the only thing I've ever wanted to be.

I have to help my team figure out what the hell happened.

And what fucking part Axel played in it.

Fuck. I want to say there's no way Axe would have turned on us, but Rook and Ford both said it. They'd never have gone there if they weren't certain. I try to remember . . . try to force my brain to work, but it doesn't.

Instead, I close my eyes and drift off to sleep as a flash of Axe taunting me last week about Carys pushes through my mind.

"You gonna marry my baby momma, Sinclair?" He drops his tray of food on the table in the mess hall and sits across from me.

"Fuck off, asshole. She's not your baby momma, and she never will be." Fuck, if she has it her way, she won't be mine either.

"We'll see." The asshole smiles.

He was always being a dick, but he was never serious.

We stood side by side for three years against the rest of the world.

I trusted him with my life.

A trained killer who I never thought would turn his training on us.

A knock on the door jars me from my dream, and the nurse from earlier—Denise, I think— walks in with my dad and Carys behind her.

Tears stream down Carys's beautiful cheeks, as she rushes past Dad to stand next to my bed. An old hoodie of mine engulfs her small body, and I ache to feel her skin against mine.

To take away the shadows and fear from her gorgeous green eyes.

I want to kiss her and convince her I'll be fine, even if I don't know that yet.

I want to hold her in my arms and tell her I'm never fucking letting her go again, and I don't give a shit what she has to say about it.

She's mine.

Period.

But I don't do any of that because my blendered brain is focusing on one thing. Axel betrayed us. If I was shot— which judging by the pain in my stomach and the giant fucking bullet hole there—there's no denying it. There's only one man who could have done it.

The man on top of the roof with me.

The man who may already have a slightly unhealthy obsession with this woman.

The traitor to our team who got away.

Fuck.

She lays her hand on top of mine before I jerk it away.

My mind starts racing as my pulse riots.

She can't be here. It's not safe. "What are you doing here?"

"Cooper . . ." she pleads, but I don't respond.

I can't let her see how much I want her.

How much I need her like the fucking air I breathe.

I push a button on my bed, and a different nurse appears in the doorway. "Petty Officer?"

Carys's breath catches in her throat, and I wish I could help her breathe easier. I wish I could joke with her and ask her why it took me being shot for her to figure out what mattered. Because the look on this woman's face tells me she figured it out and finally realized just how wrong she was. But that's not how this is gonna play out.

Not now.

It can't.

Instead of doing any of that, I look at the older nurse. "I want this woman removed from my approved list. I don't want her here."

"Cooper," my dad barks.

No matter how much I wish it was different, her words on the beach from months ago tickle my brain. I need to break us now, so I don't destroy us later. She'll forgive me for this when it's over. She fucking has to.

A tear falls down Carys's cheek and hits my hand.

I force all the warmth from my face when I look at her again. "Get out."

A stubborn glint appears in her eyes as she crosses her arms over her chest, refusing to budge.

"Miss, I have to ask you to leave. Your presence here isn't good for him." I see when Carys wavers. She'd never want to hurt me, even if she already ripped out my fucking soul. What kind of fucked up karma is it that now I'm doing the same thing to her?

I close my eyes when she reaches for me and turn my

head as she runs her finger along my temple. "I'll go for now. But that doesn't mean I'm leaving you. I love you, Cooper, and I'll be back."

She's saying all the words I wanted to hear. But I can't now.

They don't change anything.

She takes a step away, before I stop her. "Carys . . ."

This beautiful girl turns her head back to me, full of hope.

"Don't bother coming back. We're done. You made sure of that two months ago." The words are bitter as they leave my lips.

Hard to say.

Even more hard to watch her hear them.

A sob wrenches from the depths of her throat as she leaves my room, more broken than when she entered. And like the asshole I am, I watch her go.

Dad curses under his breath but holds his ground next to me.

The part of my heart that fractured a month ago riots at the idea I'm causing her pain. But until I know what's going on with the team and Axe, it's better this way.

Once the nurse follows Carys out, Dad turns to me, utter exhaustion settling deeply in the lines of his face. He drags a chair across the worn tile floor and sits down next to my bed. "How are you feeling, son?" I know he's got more to say, but he doesn't . . . *yet*.

He takes my hand in his, in a way he hasn't done since I was young, and squeezes it.

"Like I've been shot," I try to joke, but judging by the look on his face, it falls flat. "Too soon?"

"We thought you were captured. We thought you were dead." His face pales with his words. "So, yeah . . . Too soon, Cooper."

His words hurt more than the pounding in my head. "Sorry, Dad. I'm sorry you had to go through that."

"I don't need an apology. I just need to know you're okay. Jesus . . ." he groans. "You've taken ten years off my life during the past forty-eight hours. What happened?"

There's no way I can tell him what's going on, even if I remembered all of it.

I'm still a Navy SEAL, and there are rules for a reason.

It takes me a minute to get my thoughts straight. "I'm not sure what happened, Dad. But there are things going on with the team. I need you to take Carys and leave Germany. Go home. It's safer for both of you there."

"Safer?" he questions. "What are you talking about? Are you still in danger, son?"

I close my eyes and try to fight back the nausea churning in my stomach. "I'm not sure what's going on yet. And I couldn't tell you even if I knew. The thing is, I need you safe, so I need you to leave." I close my eyes and lean my head back against my pillow as I breathe through the dizziness and nausea that are hitting me hard. "I need you to take Carys home."

"Carys is an entirely different conversation, Coop. Why would you hide that from us?" Even with my eyes closed, I can feel the disappointment radiating off him in waves, and I suddenly feel like I did when Nattie and I were ten years old and were about to get in trouble. Except Declan isn't here to save me.

"Dad . . ." I struggle to find the right words. "I'm sorry I didn't tell you sooner, but—"

"You didn't tell me at all," he barks roughly, and my eyes shoot to his. "She stood up to the entire family and demanded to come here because she's in love with you. And let me tell you, your sister and Murphy didn't go easy on her. But she did it anyway, so she could be here. *With you*. And you just threw her out." Dad's voice might still be full of love, but I can't miss the judgment in his words.

I'm not sure whether it's anger or hurt or a mixture of both.

"I raised you to be a better man than that, son."

"Then keep her safe until I can do it myself, and I promise to show you what kind of man I really am." I grab his arm. "Please, Dad." My vision blurs as I think about what kind of shitstorm we're all walking into once we can finally all walk again. "Take her home."

"I think you're doing the wrong thing, Cooper." He stands from the chair, and I'm pretty sure he's telling me no. "I'll check her in at the hotel, but neither of us is leaving until I'm sure you're going to be okay. Don't bother fighting me." He leans down and kisses my head the way he kisses Callen. "I love you."

"You need to go back to Kroydon Hills, Dad. It's safer for everyone that way. Me included. I can't take care of the shit I need to handle if you're here." My frustration grows with every minute he pushes back.

His eyes soften. "I've got news for you, kid. You're not handling anything for a few days. Not in the shape you're in. Get some sleep." He takes a step back. "I'll see you tomorrow, Cooper. I'll try to keep Carys away, but I'm not making any promises."

The door closes behind my father, and Trick opens the curtain between us with some kind of remote. "You've got to keep her away. We have no idea what Axe's up to. And seriously man, he's already infatuated with your girl. Better to piss her off now and fix it later than to put her on his radar any more than she already is."

"If he wants us, she's my biggest weakness." I lean my head back and close my eyes, wondering how we got here.

CARYS

I TRY TO HOLD MY HEAD UP AND PUT ONE FOOT IN FRONT OF the other as I walk down the hospital corridor, but my heart breaks a little more with each step that takes me further from Cooper.

I did this to us. I broke us then, so I wouldn't destroy us later.

That's been my mantra.

It's what's gotten me through the tsunami of regret I've been drowning in for months.

I pushed him away, thinking I was doing the right thing.

I've never been so damn wrong about anything in my life.

Never.

But Cooper was right about one thing, and shame on me for not realizing it now.

I should have fought harder for him. For us. My heart cracks when I realize I gave up on us so easily. I thought I knew what was best. I didn't. It only took one moment of thinking I'd lost him forever for me to accept what I already knew deep down. I fucked up, and now I need to fix it.

Even if it's the last thing I do.

Once I get back to the waiting room, I take a seat in the far corner and pull up the photo app on my phone. This has been my favorite form of self-torture for a few weeks, but it feels different now. I'm not longing for what could have been, like I've been doing. Now I'm looking at the images of us, determined to figure out how to repair what I've broken.

After a few minutes, I switch over to my text messages and open my chat with Jessie.

Carys: Are you coming to Germany?
Jessie: No. Ford told me to stay put. How are you doing? How's Cooper?
Carys: Cooper's pretty banged up. Coach is with him now. I'll be okay once I know more.
Jessie: Can I do anything?
Carys: Do you have a time machine? Because he doesn't want anything to do with me.
Jessie: I don't believe that.
Carys: He sent me away, Jess. He didn't even want me in the room.
Jessie: Don't give up. Our men have to believe they're invincible. It's part of their DNA. They don't do well with being reminded they're human and break like the rest of us. He'll come around.
Carys: I hope you're right. How's Emerson?
Jessie: She's refusing to get out of bed. But I've got her. You take care of our guys, and I'll take care of our girl.
Carys: Love you, Jess.
Jessie: Love you too, Carys.

I stare at my screensaver. It's a picture of Coop and me from New Year's Eve. A selfie I took as we huddled under the blankets while the fireworks over the ocean lit up the night. I'm looking at the camera, but Coop . . . Coop's looking at me. His blue eyes are filled with nothing but love. Such a far stretch from the hate I saw in them today.

It might not be easy, but I know I can fix this.

It's a good thing I've never been scared of hard work.

I must have fallen asleep because I'm startled awake and nearly scream in Coach's face as my heart threatens to beat out of my chest. "Oh my God. You scared me, Coach."

"Sorry, kiddo." He offers me his hand and pulls me to my feet. "Come on. Let's go get checked in at the hotel."

"How is he, Coach?" My voice trembles a little, even though I try to maintain the control I've been fighting for.

Coach looks back in the direction he came from, hesitating. "He's tired. But he's going to be okay." I'm not sure if he's trying to convince himself or me as he wraps an arm around my shoulders and guides me toward the door. "They were taking him down for an MRI when I was leaving. I'll come back later tonight to check on him."

Another fissure rips through my heart.

He'll be coming back alone.

I shouldn't be surprised, but the anguish I feel at the reality nearly takes me to my knees.

Cooper doesn't want to see me. He doesn't forgive me.

The hotel is a short walk from the hospital under a cloud-covered gray sky.

Fitting for my mood.

Once we're inside, it takes no time for us to check in under the reservation Mom made. Thankfully, she was thinking ahead.

We push through the door of the two-bedroom suite, both of us exhausted.

Emotionally and physically.

The space is bigger than Coach and I need. A living room and kitchenette sit between two bedrooms with a large window overlooking the street below. I cross the room and push the curtain aside to see the hospital staring back at me.

I can't help but think I should still be there.

Coach carries my small bag into one of the bedrooms and rests it on a chair by another window. He stares out for a second, no doubt looking at the hospital like I just did, before turning around and yawning. His dark-blue eyes are rimmed in red with dark circles underneath, betraying a soul-deep exhaustion. He wraps his strong arms around me, and I lose every ounce of strength I've fought so hard to maintain.

The dam holding back my emotions finally buckles from the mounting pressure, and big, fat tears stream down my face, soaking his jacket as a guttural sob lodges in my throat.

Coach holds me while sobs wrack my body.

"I'm sorry," I tell him through a mix of tears and snot.

I'm a mess.

I pull back and wipe my face on my sleeve. "These aren't all sad tears. He's alive. I don't know if I truly believed it until I saw him for myself."

"I know. I didn't want to leave." He rubs soothing circles on my back while I fight to calm myself down. "Everyone tells you it gets easier once your kids grow up, but they're wrong. At least when they were little, we knew where they were. I'd rest my hand on their backs while they were sleeping, just to feel them breathe."

I hiccup. "I need to feel him breathe, Coach. I'm sorry.

24

I'm sure you don't want to hear that, especially after you saw how much I've hurt him. But my God, I want to feel him breathe."

Coach pulls away from me and bends his knees, so we're eye level. "Listen to me, Carys. Don't give up on him yet. Okay? Give him some space for now. But don't give up."

"How?" The one-word slips past my lips as I cry. "He doesn't want me here, Coach."

"There's always a way, if you want it bad enough."

But how many odds are already stacked against us?

COOPER

"She's sat in the waiting room for the last two days, son. She's been helping Emerson make arrangements for Linc. Your team leader's wife and Carys have been taking care of things for her." My heart hurts for my friend who's never going to get to meet his baby, and my blood pressure soars when I think about Axe pulling the trigger.

And worse, I'm having a hard time accepting that Linc's gone and Axe is the cause. My psyche refuses to believe it, and my blendered brain isn't helping because I can't remember it.

"You're really not going to see her before we leave? Maybe it would help if you talked." My father stands at the foot of my bed, arms crossed over his chest. His eyes are pinched in annoyance.

I don't blame him.

I can't give him more information, and he's not listening to what I do say.

I wanted him to leave as soon as he got here three days ago.

To take Carys and go back to Kroydon Hills, far away from this clusterfuck.

He insisted he wasn't going anywhere until I was cleared by the doctor.

But it doesn't look like that's happening yet, and the doc won't tell me how long it's going to take.

"No, Dad. Carys can't come back here." I hold his eyes and make sure he feels the strength of my words. "She can't be here."

"Cooper, I try not to meddle. Especially considering I love you both. But I have to say this one thing." His posture loosens, and he takes a step closer. "Love is messy, son. Carys was knocked down hard with her diagnosis. She knows pushing you away was wrong. You owe it to her to hear her out, at the very least."

"Like she talked to me?" I bite back.

I still love her.

I always will.

But when all this is over, I'm gonna spank her ass for pushing me away.

Dad stares at me, waiting me out for a better answer.

"We'll talk at some point, Dad. But it won't be here, and it can't be now." There's no way for me to protect her here. "You guys have already been here too long. You've got to go home."

Dad wraps his arms around me in a tight embrace. "I love you, kid. I want to hear from you as soon as the doc comes in with another update. Got it?"

"I'll call as soon as I can." He moves the rolling table over until it's next to the bed, then hands me my phone.

"Make sure you answer your sister. She's driving me crazy." Dad shakes his head like all of us do when it comes to my persistent twin when she gets mad.

God help the man who gets in her way.

Guess that's Brady's problem now.

"No electronics, remember?" I really don't think I can handle getting into it with Nat yet. Not when my brain still feels like scrambled eggs.

"Coop, she's pregnant with twins. If she doesn't hear

from you soon, she's getting on a plane and flying over here to see you for herself. Will you please just call her?" He turns and grabs his coat from the chair, then waits.

"Fine. But if she yells, I'm hanging up." She's going to yell. We both know it. Nattie is never quiet.

Dad crosses his arms over his thick chest and tries to act annoyed again but fails. "Love you, son. I'll call when we land."

"Dad . . . take care of Carys." I hope one day she understands why I did this.

Dad shakes his head. "Don't underestimate her, son. That girl is stronger than you think."

There's a knock on the door, followed by Ford's head sticking in. "Hey, brother." He glances between Dad and me. "Sorry, we didn't mean to interrupt."

"You're not interrupting," Dad claps Ford's back, as he shakes his hand. "Just do me a favor and make sure he calls his sister before you're all stuck having to deal with her." He looks back at me one more time before walking through the door, and the immediate relief I have, knowing that he and Carys will be on a jet within a few hours, has my shoulders sagging.

Ford laughs as Rook and he stroll into the room in their full uniforms.

Rook closes the door and leans against it with his hands shoved in his pockets. Ford clears his throat. "Listen, Rook and I are being sent stateside later today."

The words he left unsaid are that Trick and I won't be going back to base with them.

The injuries to Trick's leg are severe and could take months of physical therapy. That's a one-way ticket back to Coronado. And head injuries are tricky. My vision isn't even back to 100 percent yet.

The words *potential medical discharge* still echo in my shaky brain from my conversation with the neuro doc they brought in yesterday.

Potential permanent partial loss of vision.

I haven't told the guys yet. I want to know more first.

"We're needed for debriefing and . . ." Ford trails off.

"And?" I prompt.

He looks between Trick and me. "For Linc's funeral."

Acid churns in my gut. "Then I'm going too." He was my best fucking friend.

"Same," Trick backs me.

"Neither of you are medically cleared to travel." Ford's gaze slams into me. "Maybe by next week . . ."

Rook claps a hand on my shoulder. "We'll need you in top form, brother."

My diagnosis sours my stomach, twisting my guts. "Fucking bullshit" is all I finally mutter.

"We'll be in touch as soon as we get more intel. Just focus on getting yourselves where you need to be to get the hell out of here." Ford grasps my hand in a firm shake.

"Carys . . ." I let her name hang in the air. But he knows what I'm asking.

"Already done, brother. Jessie's been talking to her and keeping me in the loop. I'll have eyes on her as soon as she gets back to California."

"Phoenix will keep an eye on her until then. Who the fuck knows where Axe's head's at, or what he's gonna try?" Rook adds.

"She's going to California?" I groan, frustrated. I thought she'd be staying in Kroydon Hills. An entire country away from this shit.

"Jessie said she's coming to help Emerson." He shifts uncomfortably. "Em's not handling everything well. We should have more for you guys soon." Ford steps away and claps Trick's shoulder before they walk out the door.

This is all so fucked.

CARYS

COACH TURNS DOWN THE COBBLESTONE STREETS OF OLD City, less than thirty minutes after the Kingston jet lands back in Philly. I feigned sleep during most of the flight home, not ready to hear Coach's latest words of wisdom.

He means well, but sometimes a girl just wants to wallow in her own pity party.

And I'm throwing myself a hell of a good one tonight.

Not a single star lights up the dark night's sky as I say goodnight to Coach and climb out of the car in front of Chloe's townhouse. It's as if even the heavens know it isn't a good night . . . That I'm not supposed to be in Kroydon Hills.

My heart is still in Germany, and that's where my soul longs to be. Even sitting in that waiting room, knowing Cooper hated me, was better than closing the door behind myself as I walk into the townhouse.

This feels too final.

And I'm not ready for final.

I lock the door, then take a few steps toward the kitchen for a bottle of water before I stop dead in my tracks.

Chloe and a stunning woman with long jet-black hair are locked in a hot embrace. The leggy bombshell is leaning against the fridge with her head thrown back, while Chloe's lips skim her neck, and her hand works inside the front of her shorts.

"Oh, shit. Sorry," I mumble as I scramble away.

"Carys, wait," Chloe's voice calls out.

Refusing to stop, I shake my head. "I can't, Chloe. We'll talk in the morning." I don't look back as I drag my body up the stairs, drop my bag on the floor, and face-plant in my bed.

The last thing I see behind my closed eyelids before falling to sleep is the look of disgust on Cooper's face as he threw me out of his room.

"Carys . . ." Daphne's voice invades my sleep-deprived brain.

I ignore it and burrow deeper in my bed, not sure what time it is as my blanket is tugged down my body. Cool air washes over my skin, but I am most definitely not ready to face the day. I tossed and turned all night and doubt I got more than an hour or two of actual sleep. And as much as I love my best friend, Daphne's voice is not welcome right now.

Dream or not.

I crack one eye open, protesting the wakeup call, to find my bestie sitting next to me. Looking perfectly put together, her blonde hair pulled back and her pearls resting against her throat.

I don't have the energy to deal with her right now, so I shove my pillow over my head instead. "What do you want?"

She pulls my pillow away, then lays her head down on it next to me with a soft smile. "How are you?"

I'm not at all sure how to answer that.

"He hates me, D." The words are like acid burning my

throat as I force them out. "And the thing is, I can't even blame him." I turn my head toward her. "My eyes are dry from lack of sleep, and I'm probably dehydrated from the number of tears I've shed. He threw me out of his room, and I ended up spending the week in the waiting room, hoping he'd change his mind. Which, side note, he didn't. So basically, I'm batting a thousand."

She links her pinky with mine, the way we've done since we were little kids, but it no longer comforts me like it used to. *Adulting sucks.* "So, what are we going to do about it?"

"I'm not sure." I close my eyes, dreading the next thing I have to do. "First, I have to fly to California. I need to be there for Emerson." A fresh wave of sorrow washes over me. "The services for Linc are next week. Jessie said Em moved back in with Jack and Theo for the time being, so I'm going to stay with them for a few weeks." A tear trickles down my face, and I rest my head against D's.

She rubs her thumb over my cheek, wiping away my tears. "Okay. How about *you* get a shower, and *I* make the coffee? And then, we'll come up with a plan." She cocks an eyebrow and waits me out, knowing she's going to get her way.

"Fine." I sit up and glare. "But I want tea, not coffee. And you better have brought some Sweet Temptations muffins with you."

She shoves my shoulder as she stands from the bed. "Nope. No muffins. But I did better. I brought cupcakes."

"Vanilla bean?"

She glares. "Of course I got vanilla bean for your boring, skinny ass. Now stop stalling and tell me I'm the best bestie ever."

"I love you, D." I look at my best friend . . . really look at her. It wasn't too long ago that I was dragging *her* out of bed, and now she's got everything she's ever wanted.

The only thing I want is half a world away.

"You're going to get through this, C. And we'll be holding your hand every step of the way."

By dinnertime, I'm more grateful than I've ever been for my tribe. I'm showered, dressed, and booked on the red-eye back to San Diego later tonight. I'm not sure I'd have accomplished any of it without them.

"Carys, don't you own any black?" Daphne walks out of my closet, holding a navy-blue shirt. "This could work for a funeral."

Chloe rolls her eyes at Daphne. "You realize that's a shirt, right?" She hands me a pair of black patent-leather Mary Jane heels to add to my suitcase before she steps out of the room.

"What?" Daphne holds up the shirt and shrugs when it only grazes the tops of her thighs. "Whatever. You're shorter than me. Make it work." She shoves the hanger at me, and I throw the shirt down on the bed. "Do you know how long you're staying in San Diego?"

I shake my head. "Emerson's due in a few weeks. I think I'm at least staying until the baby's born. From what Jessie's told me, she's not doing well. And she hasn't returned any of my calls. I'm worried about her and want to be there as long as she needs me."

A charcoal-gray dress is shoved into my hands when Chloe walks back in. "Here. This should fit you."

There's a knock downstairs at the front door before it

cracks open, and a voice carries up to us. "Chloe . . . where are you?" Nattie calls out.

My eyes fly to Chloe in shock. I assumed Nattie would be back in Maryland with Brady.

"Up here, Nat." Chloe mouths the word *Sorry* to me before Nattie makes it up the stairs. I understand why she apologized when Nattie stops at the threshold of the room and her eyes lock with mine.

Anger and hurt war with each other in those blue eyes that are identical to Cooper's, and I brace myself. Not sure if I can take any more hits.

She takes in the dress in my hands, then scans the room. "Where are you going?" Her tone is snarky at best and cruel at worst.

"Nat," Chloe starts, but I step forward instead, effectively cutting her off.

"Say it, Nat. Say whatever you've got to say." I remind myself that she's my stepsister . . . Cooper's twin, who we lied to for months. And she found out in the most horrific way imaginable.

But I will not be anyone's punching bag, not today, when I'm beating myself up already.

She takes a shaky step next to me and stares before she sniffs, and her entire body shakes. "Have you talked to him? He won't answer my calls."

I shake my head and watch, glued to my spot, as Nattie drops down onto my bed and hides her face behind her hands, crying. "I'm sorry, Carys. I was horrible to you last week."

I tuck my hands under my legs, nervously looking between Chloe and Daphne as they walk out of the room. Wishing I could beg them not to leave us alone.

Nattie and I have never been close.

I doubt we ever will be.

She may only be two years older than me, but she was always Aiden's friend, and I was just his little sister. Never quite a part of their group. I tentatively reach out and lay my hand on Nat's leg, palm up.

She immediately places her palm in mine.

"It was the worst day of my life, Nat. And I'm not going to lie and say the way you and Aiden reacted didn't hurt. But I get it. Cooper and I kept something from all of you. You were entitled to feel however you felt. And none of us were in the right place to be more careful with our words. I wish it hadn't happened that way. I wish things were different."

"Why?" She squeezes my hand, and I all but yelp on the tight grip she's got on me. "Why did you guys keep it from everyone?" Then a choked sob catches in her throat. "Why did he keep it from me?"

"Nat, I . . ." I take a soothing breath in, then slowly blow it out.

Now's my chance to do this the way it should have been done, instead of making an announcement to the entire family at the worst possible moment. "I swear it came from a good place. We wanted to see what was between us before we brought you all into it. We didn't want everyone's opinions to color our feelings. And if we tried and it didn't work out, we didn't want anyone to know. Why make everything harder if we were never meant to be?"

"And are you?" Her big blue eyes blink at me, and I have to hold back my own tears when I realize I don't know how to answer her. "Are you meant to be?"

"I love him with every fiber of my being, and I always will, but it's complicated. I thought I was doing it for him . . ." I stop myself, not sure I want to give her that piece of us. "I fucked up, and I don't know how to fix it. And now, he won't even talk to me." I refuse to cry another tear as they burn the back of my eyelids. "But I'm going to do what I didn't do before, and I'm going to fight for him."

"Can I give you one piece of advice, Carys?" Both of her brows lift as she waits for my answer.

"I'm all ears."

She clasps my hand in both of hers and holds them together on her lap. Her grip even tighter now than before. "Don't give up. My brother is the most stubborn person I've ever known. So, you've got to be ready for the fight of your life if you want him to see what's right in front of him. But if you love him . . . let me tell you, it's worth the fight."

The fight of my life.

It feels more like a fight *for* my life.

COOPER

"I'M AFRAID THE 10 PERCENT LOSS OF VISION IN YOUR RIGHT eye is permanent, Petty Officer." My neurologist stands at the foot of the bed with a tablet in his hand and a pitying expression on his face.

"What do you mean permanent?" Twelve days of sitting in this hospital must be fucking with my hearing, not just my eyesight, because there's no way I just heard the doctor right. "It doesn't seem that bad."

"The loss of vision in your right eye is permanent. It's not uncommon with this type of injury. It could have been significantly worse than 10 percent. The good news is it's only one eye, and your body will naturally compensate for it." The *but* is coming. It's in his stance and in his voice. "However, that does put you below the minimum sight requirement for the Navy."

The blow hits harder than any suicide bomber ever could. "You're telling me I'm done."

"I'm telling you you're being medically discharged. You've done your duty honorably. You're being sent back to Coronado to sign off on the final paperwork. You won't be returning to duty." He hands me my hospital discharge papers. "You have a flight to catch."

He walks out of the room as detached as he walked in, leaving me there to deal with the bomb he just dropped. Kind of fitting since an actual explosion caused the damage in the first place.

I've spent my life wanting to be a SEAL.

I've worked toward it.

I've fought for it.

I loved it.

It's who I am. Who I *was*.

My phone rings next to me, and I pick it up without thinking. "What?"

"Real nice way to answer the phone, Cooper Sinclair."

Shit. It's my sister.

I've avoided Nattie for the past week. Guess my time's up. "Nat, it's not a good time."

"It hasn't been a good time for nearly two weeks, Coop. I've called you every day. Every. Single. Day. Asshole. You almost died. You seriously couldn't take ten minutes to call me back? *Hey, sis, I'm okay. Hey sis, I love you too. Hey, sis, I've been banging our stepsister and keeping it from you.* I mean, you had so many options, Coop. You could have picked any of them." She finally takes a breath, and I jump in.

"Listen, how about this? *Hey, sis, I just got told I've got 10 percent permanent loss of vision, and my naval career is over.* Does that work for you? I love you. But trust me when I say now is not a good time. I'll call you back soon." I end the call before she can say anything else. Not ready . . . for any of it.

Three hours later, I've signed away my life just to get discharged from the hospital, and I'm having a hard time reconciling my new reality as I get ready to head back to the states, less than the man I was when I left. This was it. The goal. My plan for my life. Career military.

Seventy-five percent of the men who start BUD/S don't finish.

That was never an option for me.

I worked my ass off for this, and now it's gone.

And who the fuck am I if I'm not a SEAL?

The thoughts play on a constant loop in my mind.

Trick wheels himself back through the door after physical therapy but stops when he sees me zipping my bag. His face pinches as he watches me throw my duffle over my shoulder. "You getting out today?"

"Yeah, man. They cleared me an hour ago. I'm catching a flight home tonight."

"Fuck," he groans. "They made it official?"

I nod, a mix of anger and regret churning in a wicked current in my gut. "An hour ago. Honorable medical discharge. My vision will never be what the Navy needs again."

"At least you'll be back in time for Linc's funeral." He grabs the chocolate pudding cup from my uneaten lunch tray and rips it open. "They still don't know when they're sending me stateside for rehab. Should be soon. But who the fuck knows if I'll ever be back on the teams again." He shoves the pudding-covered spoon into his mouth. "Have you heard anything else from Rook or Ford?" Pudding slips out of the corner of his mouth.

"Dude, fucking swallow first."

Trick's whole face lights up. "That's what *she* said."

I laugh my first real laugh since I woke up in this place. "Whatever, dipshit. I talked to Ford. Rook's brothers haven't been able to locate Axel or the guys they think he was working with yet. There's been no communication from the terrorist group, and Command hasn't said a damn thing about anything."

He puts his spoon down and gets serious. "I'm really fucking sorry, brother."

"Yeah. Me too." I throw an arm around him and pound his back, not sure when the next time I'll see him will be. "You take care of yourself over here. Keep your eyes open, and don't fucking trust anyone. I'll make sure we read you in on everything we find."

"I guess that means you already know what you're doing when you get back to San Diego."

"Yeah," I growl. "Finding that traitorous motherfucker and making sure he pays."

My military flight landed two hours ago. And thanks to the ever-efficient Navy, my separation paperwork has been signed.

I'm no longer employed by the United States Navy.

I also have no way to get the fuck home, so I call Ford.

My incision is on fire from sitting on a plane for so damn long, and my new constant—a headache forged in the fires of hell—is pounding behind my eyes as he pulls up in front of me and rolls down the window. "I bet I could make a lot of money as an Uber driver."

"Worth a try." I reach for my wallet and throw a dollar through the window.

"Get the fuck in the car, Sinclair." He navigates us out of the parking lot before turning off the radio. "Is it true?"

I silence the phone ringing in my pocket. "You heard?"

"Yeah, man. Trick called earlier. This fuckin' sucks. I'm sorry." Traffic moves slowly as we get stuck in mid-day congestion, and exhaustion kicks in.

Understatement of the century. "Me too. Tell me you've at least got an update on Axel."

Ford shakes his head. "We're still working on it. But there hasn't been any movement."

"He's one of us. He's as good as us. We're not going to find him if he doesn't want to be found." I close my eyes and lean back against the seat as my head pounds harder.

Ford takes the hint, and we drive the rest of the way in silence. When we pull into the driveway of Trick's house, I open my eyes to see Ford staring at me. "You know Linc's services are tomorrow, right?"

"I do now. I wasn't sure." I open the door and grab my duffle. "Thanks for the ride. I'll see you tomorrow."

"Let me know if you need anything."

I nod and slam the door shut just as my fucking phone vibrates again. Dad's name flashes across the screen as I let myself into the house. "Hey, Dad."

"Your sister said you were discharged." Okay then.

I guess we're skipping the niceties.

"Yeah. Ten percent loss of vision puts me over the acceptable limit for any visual deficiency. I just finished signing the paperwork . . . so I guess I'm now unemployed." Nothing like Nattie running to Dad.

"Oh, Cooper. I'm so sorry, son. Nattie only said you were being discharged from the hospital. I didn't know . . ." He hesitates, not sure what to say.

That makes two of us.

"Why don't you come home for a while. Recoup here. You could stay with us."

I'm thinking *Hell no* would not be an acceptable answer. "I appreciate it, Dad. But I'm already back in Coronado. I have some things I need to handle. I'm not sure how long it's gonna take."

"The offer is always there, son."

"Thanks, Dad. We'll talk soon, okay?" I walk through the door of the house I shared with Trick and Linc, and everything feels wrong. "I gotta go, Dad." I don't wait for him to answer before I end the call.

The house is quiet. The air inside is untouched and stale, but something feels off.

I drop my bag in my bedroom and quickly check out the rest of the rooms, leaving Linc's for last. His door is open, and I'm not sure what I'm expecting to find. It's empty. He and Emerson had gotten their own place before we were deployed. He wanted space for the baby.

My fucking chest hurts at the insanity of it all.

Linc's gone because of Axel.

What the actual fuck?

I make my way to the kitchen, knowing there's nothing in the fridge, but the vodka in the freezer should be as good as new and ice fucking cold. I consider grabbing a glass for a second, then decide the bottle will do just fine and crack it open.

Maybe this can take away the fucked up thoughts that won't leave me the hell alone.

The guilt.

The anger.

The fucking hate.

One minute, I was sleeping. The next, I'm drowning.

At least I think I am.

I sit up quickly to a spinning room and a sharp pain in my side while water drips down my face and soaks my shirt. My brain takes a minute to catch up to my eyes when I see Rook standing next to me in his full uniform. His dress whites are freshly pressed, with his medals lining his chest and an empty glass in his hand. "What the hell, man?"

"Get moving, Sinclair." He kicks my foot. "I've been trying to get you up for five fucking minutes. We're going to be late, and you can't show up to Linc's funeral smelling like you bathed in Russia's finest."

Fuck . . . I stand on unsteady legs, nearly tripping over the empty bottle of vodka on the floor next to my feet. I feel about as good as a beaten dog when I lean down to pick the bottle up, my side screaming with pain while my head throbs in unison.

Great fucking job, Sinclair.

Linc would be especially proud of the way I honored his memory last night.

When I stand up, Rook stares me down. Not an easy feat when not even an inch separates our heights. "You done feeling sorry for yourself yet, or are you enjoying the self-pity? Cause I gotta tell you, I liked you a fuck of a lot better when you were a cocky little shit."

"Fuck you, brother." I throw the bottle in the trash and slam the door of the bathroom behind me.

When I turn the shower on and wait for the hot water to kick in, I hear him yell, "Make sure you shave that shit off your face too. You look like a teenager trying to grow his first beard."

Family comes in all sorts of shapes and sizes. And sometimes they're the only ones who are willing to tell you what you need to hear even if you don't want to admit they're right. One night of feeling like shit for myself was more than I should have indulged in.

I'm alive.

We don't all get to be here and say that.

CARYS

I always knew I've led a charmed life.

Okay, so my dad's an asshole who forgot Aiden and I existed after he divorced my mom, but I barely remember him as more than a blip on my radar. I've been loved and protected. And while yes, I've buried both my grandparents in recent years, they lived until ripe old ages, and both passed in their sleep from natural causes.

This is the first time I've ever been to a funeral for someone my age.

Someone young and healthy.

A new husband who would have become a father in just a few weeks, had he gotten the chance to live that long.

And as I sit here, with my arm wrapped around Emerson—who's had silent tears pouring from her eyes from the moment we got into the limo—I realize just how lucky I am, lupus and all, just to be alive.

Em and Jack's mom and dad both flew in for the funeral, meeting us at the house this morning before we were all ushered into the waiting vehicles. But it's my hand Em reached for as she slid across the back seat. "Just us and Jack and Theo," she whispers.

I lean my head out of the car. "Jack."

He turns to me, dressed in a crisp black suit, running his hand through his dark hair. He looks tired. We all do. He takes a few steps toward me, and I whisper, "Just you and Theo, okay?"

Jack agrees and says something to his parents before he taps Theo, and the two of them climb into the back with us.

Emerson doesn't bother wiping away her tears. "Shut the door, please. I don't want Mom and Dad fighting in front of me today. I already heard her complaining that Dad brought his girlfriend, and I just can't handle it. Not today." It's the most words I've heard her speak since I got back to San Diego.

Jack pulls the door shut and rubs Em's belly. "We got you, Emmie. Whatever you need."

"I need to not be burying my husband," she says through a sob and lays her head on Jack's shoulder. Then she whispers, "But we can't always have what we need."

Jack and I walk on either side of Emerson with Theo behind her. We're a wall of support for her as we guide her toward our seats at the cemetery. Linc wasn't an overly religious man, so Em opted for a graveside service rather than a big church mass. But when the four of us stand in front of our seats and the grip Em has on my hand tightens, so does the grip Cooper has on my heart.

He's standing across from me with Rook, Ford, and Jessie. He looks incredible in his uniform, and I have to swallow down my own sob at the excruciating pain of being so close to him and knowing he doesn't want to be near me.

Is this what it felt like for him when I pushed him away?

Emerson's parents stand behind us, and Jack nods

toward the minister, answering the silent question and letting him know he can begin the ceremony.

A chill wracks my body as a team of Naval personnel remove Linc's casket from the hearse and follow the military minister to the gravesite. They secure the casket, and an American flag is stretched over the top of it.

The first tears begin stinging the backs of my eyes when the sun catches the bright blues and reds of the flag, and I feel Emerson steel her spine next to me.

Once we're all seated, she rubs her baby bump and winces, worrying me.

"Are you feeling okay?" I lay my hand over her belly and am immediately kicked by the baby.

Em looks at me with nearly lifeless eyes. "I'm not in labor yet. She's just shoving her foot into my rib cage."

I pull my hand away, but she grabs it and lays it back over her bump, linking our fingers together.

Two years ago, we were decorating our dorms and drinking at fraternity parties.

A year ago, we were both falling in love with these men.

Now, we're burying Linc, and Cooper and I might as well be in two different countries.

The minister goes through the brief service, and Ford gives a beautiful eulogy. Through it all, my eyes continuously stray to Cooper. He never removes his aviators, so I don't get so much as a glimpse of his eyes. But I feel them on me, as soft as a lover's touch. He might be mad, but there's no way this man can hate me. And when the SEALs standing with Bravo team all bang their Trident pins into the casket, leaving Cooper for last, my heart catches in my throat . . . again.

I refuse to give up on us.

I'll never give up on *him*.

It's as if I lived my entire life in a dull black-and-white

movie until he introduced me to the excitement of color. Then I threw it away and stepped back into the gray. But I'm not giving up on us. I screwed up, but I can fix it. I have to believe that.

The minister asks us to stand again, and the riflemen are signaled for the twenty-one-gun salute. With each ringing of the guns, my body jolts, and I strengthen my resolve to fight for what's mine. And as long as there's a breath left in my body, that man is mine.

COOPER

"ARE YOU GOING TO TALK TO HER?"

I turn my head toward Jessie, who just walked outside with a plate of food in her hand.

"Come on, Coop. You need to eat something. Hanger is a real thing." She shoves the food at me, then stands in front of me, waiting. Always the military wife, making sure everyone else is fine and has what they need. "Take it, Coop. I'm betting you're still on heavy duty medication, and you need to eat." One eyebrow raises.

"Why are you mothering me instead of your husband?" I fire back at her.

A small smile tugs at her lips. "He's inside talking to Stone Madden. I decided I didn't want to watch him revert back to a teenage boy, fangirling over his idol, and came to find you."

"Thanks." I take the plate from her and sit down, just as I see Jack place his hand on Carys's back and whisper in her ear. Her brown hair brushes against his face, and when she turns, she stops and stares at me for a moment before she moves up the stairs of the back deck to go into the house.

"Are you going to tell her why you're pushing her away?" Jessie sits down next to me and watches Carys. "She loves you. Today of all days, I think we should hold on to that where we can, Cooper."

Her words hit hard.

She's not wrong.

"Carys is safer the further away from me she is. We have no idea what the hell's going on, Jess. Ford *had* to tell you. You're his wife. Carys is better off not knowing." I'm not sure if I'm trying to convince Jessie or myself.

"Is *she* safer, or are *you*, Coop?" Her hand moves to her hip. "You guys like to think you can protect us from everything. But that's not what we want. Ford told me because I'm his partner. He told me so I could be aware. Prepared."

"That's the thing, Jess," I cut her off. "She and I aren't partners. When I wanted to be there for her . . . to be the one she leaned on, talked to . . . fucking trusted—" I stop myself and look away. I stare out over the ocean as it crashes against the sand and then stand. "We're not partners, Jess. So she doesn't get a say in how I protect her."

I excuse myself and walk into the house, going in search of the coffee I saw some guests walking around with. Once I'm in the kitchen, it's as if there's a fucking beacon above my head that says I don't want to be left alone, and everyone stops in to talk. A few of the guys from Delta team check in before Theo pours himself a cup of coffee and leans against the island.

Great.

Another person ready to give me their two cents.

"I was glad to hear you were okay, man." The drummer stands there with his suit coat forgotten somewhere and the sleeves of his white dress shirt rolled up his arms. He's cut his hair shorter than it was a few months ago, and there's a tattoo on his forearm that wasn't there before. The muscles under his tat move as he spins a serving spatula through his fingers like a drumstick. "You gonna be in town for a while?"

"I'm not sure what I'm doing yet, but I should be here

for a few weeks," I answer noncommittally, not sure why he's asking.

"You know, Carys is planning on staying for a few weeks too. The band is going on tour."

"That's really great, man. Congratulations." At least something good is happening for someone.

"Yeah well, we leave in two days. We're opening for Black Stone, and according to Stone, the show must go on. Anyway, Carys was already planning on staying through the end of October. So, I figured maybe you'd . . . I don't know. I guess I figured you'd want to know."

As if she knew we were talking about her, the love of my fucking life appears in front of me, close enough to touch but a million miles away. She's changed out of the pretty dress from earlier, but she's as beautiful as ever. Her red-rimmed eyes scan me from the top of my head to the tips of my shiny black shoes before she turns them to Theo. "Hey, if you see Jack, can you let him know Em's sleeping?"

"Yeah. No problem." He kisses the top of her head, then juts his chin toward me. "See ya later, Coop."

Carys slips into Theo's vacated spot next to me, leaning back against the island.

She shouldn't look amazing in sweatpants and a sweater, but she does. It's got one of those necklines that hits her collarbone and kisses her shoulders. There isn't a hint of cleavage to be seen, and the way it skims her subtle curves makes it seem prim and proper . . . but on Carys, it's the perfect package. "Cooper . . ." She reaches for me but drops her hand mid-air and smooths it down her legs. "How are you feeling?"

"I'll be fine," I grunt out, torn between wanting to get her as far away from here as possible and wanting to take her home with me.

She nods, not surprised by my short answer. "Have you talked to Nattie yet?"

"Yeah. We talked for a minute before I left Germany." My eye twitches from exhaustion and from the guilt of how quickly I got off the phone. "She was . . ."

"Yeah. That's probably my fault. I didn't exactly tell the family about us with any . . . finesse." She shrugs, and her sweater slips off one bare shoulder. "You're probably going to hear it at some point from Aiden too, if you haven't already."

I chuckle, staring at her exposed skin. "Yeah, Murphy's called a few times. I haven't answered. I wasn't really supposed to have electronics in the hospital."

"Cooper." She reaches up and runs her fingers over the epaulet on my shoulder and down my arm.

I want to tell her I'm sorry she had to tell them all without me.

That we'll deal with it together.

That everything will be fine.

But instead, I push her further away. "Guess telling them didn't make a difference after all," I say and then turn and walk away, feeling like a bigger ass now than I did at the hospital.

I don't say goodbye to anyone.

I just walk through the front door and down the street to my house.

I hate myself a little more with each step.

I try to force myself to believe I'm only pushing her away for her safety, but that's not entirely true, and I know it. Loving Carys was never the problem. It's still not. But I'm so fucking mad at her, I can't stand it.

I pull my key out of my pocket to open the front door of the house, but it pushes open without my unlocking it.

The door wasn't completely shut, although I'm sure I shut and locked it when I left.

Pushing it open slowly, I enter the house and clear it, room by room, grabbing my gun from my bedroom when I get there. No one's here, and there's very little out of place. However, I can tell someone has gone through my room. My duffle bag is open, and I know I zipped it closed this morning because I caught a shirt on the damn thing when I did.

Cooper: Looks like someone's been in my place. They searched my shit. But they're gone now.
Ford: Be there soon. Jessie has a shift at the hospital tonight, I gotta get her home first.
Rook: On my way.

"You're sure you zipped your bag this morning? You were pretty pissed and not paying attention when I woke you up." Rook runs the zipper back and forth as the three of us stand around the kitchen table, trying to figure out what the hell is happening.

"You threw a glass of water on me." I stare at him in frustration.

Ford fucking laughs, like that's the funniest thing he's ever heard. "No shit? You woke him up with water to the face? That's fantastic."

"You're both assholes," I grunt, while they both laugh. Then I go through my bag again, making sure there's nothing I could have missed. "I haven't gotten my stuff back from deployment yet. The only things in the bag are what I had at the hospital and what I had on me when it all happened."

Where's my feather?

I search the bag, pulling everything out, but it's not there.

"What's missing?" Ford asks as he inspects the contents after I do, while Rook walks into the living room.

"This?" Ford and I both turn to Rook, who's holding my feather in one hand as he squats in front of the couch I slept on last night, running the other hand under it.

I cross the room and grab the feather from his hand, smoothing out its soft vane. I kept my good-luck charm in an envelope inside the pocket of my uniform while I was on deployment. It was a nice surprise when I found it with my belongings while I was packing.

Rook stands up with something else in his hand. "Is this your flash drive, Sinclair? It was right next to where that damn feather fell out when you knocked your bag over this morning before your miserable ass drug it to your room."

I take the small flash drive from his hand, and a memory scratches at the back of my brain. Turning it over in my hand, I close my eyes and try to force the memory. "I don't think it's mine, but I had it." I open my eyes and look at Ford and Rook. "I think it's Axel's." Pieces of that night come back to me. "It fell out of his pocket when all hell broke loose during the op. I picked it up, and the world went black a minute later."

"Grab your laptop, Coop." Ford looks at me like I'm crazy for not moving.

"My guess is the Navy has that packed away with the rest of my shit from base that hasn't made it back yet." I look between the two of them. "Either of you have yours yet?"

Before either of us has the chance to answer, Ford's

phone rings. "Give me a second. It's Jessie." He turns his back to us. "Hey, Jess." He listens to whatever she says on the other end of the phone. "Okay. Thanks, babe. Love you." Then he turns back to us. "Emerson's in labor. She's at the hospital."

"She's not due for three weeks." Linc was counting down the days until her due date. He didn't care that everyone said babies never come on time. He checked off the days on his calendar like a kid waiting for summer vacation.

"Yeah well, tell that to the baby. Come on. We're going to the hospital." Ford pockets the flash drive. "We'll figure this shit out after we make sure Emerson and the baby are okay."

Rook holds out his palm. "Give me the flash drive. I'll go home and check it out first. Then I'll meet the two of you at the hospital with the information."

Ford passes it to him, and we all agree to meet up at the hospital.

But first, I need to change. Once the two of them leave, I get out of my dress whites and throw on a pair of jeans and a t-shirt, then make sure to lock the house up tight and set the alarm when I leave.

Time to meet the newest member of the family.

CARYS

E<small>MERSON IS STILL UPSTAIRS, SLEEPING, WHEN THE LAST OF</small> the guests, including her parents, finally leave after the service. Leaving Jack, Theo, and me sitting in the kitchen, looking around at the mess. Jack stands behind me, rubbing my shoulders, and I crack my sore neck. "Dad said he'd send a cleaning crew tomorrow morning to take care of everything." He squeezes one more time before moving to the side and helping himself to another cup of coffee from the tureen that's still warm.

"Thank God." I drop my head down onto my arms that are resting on the counter. "It's been a really long day already. I just want to go to bed."

"I second that," Theo agrees as he stands and drags his hand down his face.

"Umm . . . guys?" Emerson walks slowly down the stairs, her hair sitting in a messy bun on top of her head, and her sleep shorts and a tank doing a terrible job covering her extremely pregnant body. One hand white-knuckles the railing while the other rubs her back. "I don't think anybody is going to sleep anytime soon."

We all look at her, a little surprised to see her awake and joining us. "What's up, Em? What do you need? I'll get it," I offer, just as Jack asks the same thing.

But it's Theo who quickly darts across the room and grabs her arm, so she can lean on him.

"My water just broke." She doubles over and screams in pain, and I see the water leaking down her legs.

We all scramble, rushing Emerson into Jack's car and practically flying to the hospital. At one point, Jack blows through a red light, and I'm pretty sure he doesn't stop for a single stop sign. Em sits next to me in the back seat, sobbing when she isn't breathing through contractions. "This baby cannot come today. I can't have to celebrate my baby's birthday every year on the same day I buried him, CC. I just can't."

"It's okay." I push the messy hair that's fallen out of her bun away from her face. "Just breathe, Em. Don't worry about that now." I meet Jack's eyes through the rearview mirror, and we share a moment of concern.

Emerson has slipped into a dark place since she lost Linc. In the days since I've been back, she's barely left her room or spoken to anyone. And each of us have been taking turns trying to get her to eat. We've all hoped, with the funeral behind us, we'd be able to help her get to a better place by the time the baby came.

We thought we had a few weeks.

Looks like we thought wrong.

After I time another contraction, I look at Em hesitantly. "Should I call your mom or dad and ask them to come to the hospital? I think your mom said she wasn't flying out until tomorrow."

"No," Em snaps. "Don't call them. I just want you guys and Jessie. Please don't call my parents tonight."

"Whatever you want, Emmie. We've got you," Jack soothes his sister as he pulls up in front of the hospital, his breaks squealing as he throws the door open and commandeers a wheelchair.

It's a long night for all of us. Emerson oscillates between crying hysterically that the baby can't be coming the same day she buried Linc and begging for the baby to come, so this can all be over. I'm not sure I'll ever regain the feeling in my fingers again after the way she crushed my hand during her labor. But she does it.

Finally, with tears streaming down her face and her gut-wrenching cries filling the room, Emerson gives birth to the most beautiful baby girl I've ever seen.

A little after six in the morning, Elodie Madden-Alexander is born, screaming at the top of her lungs. And as if she already knows she comes from rock royalty, even her cries sound like the prettiest song I've ever heard.

"You did it, Em." I wipe her face with a damp cloth. "You did it, and she's beautiful."

She's tiny, barely over six pounds, with eyes so blue, they look purple, just like her momma's. Soft jet-black hair is sticking out in every direction when the nurse tries to hand her to Em, but she shakes her head no and closes her eyes.

I open my arms instead, and the nurse places her small bundled body into them. And even though I know, logically, she can't really make out my face just yet, I feel like this tiny little girl is staring into my soul.

At that moment, I make her a silent promise that Auntie Carys will always be there for her, no matter what.

I settle into a chair next to Em's bed, holding a sleeping Elodie, who's wrapped up like a baby burrito in a white hospital blanket with a big pink bow wrapped around her little head.

"Are you sure you don't want to hold her, Em?"

She looks at me with empty eyes and shakes her head. "I just want to sleep, CC."

"Okay. I've got her. You rest." We're definitely going to have to speak to someone about her depression. Em rolls to her side and pulls the blanket up.

I sit quietly watching Elodie sleep until Jack comes in, having snuck past the nurses. He takes one look at the beautiful newborn resting in my arms and steals her from me, whispering, "Go get yourself something to drink, CC. I won't go anywhere." He holds his hand up. "Scout's honor."

"Like you were ever a boy scout," I whisper.

He tips his head and runs a gentle finger down Elodie's nose. "Yeah . . . that sure as fuck wasn't happening. Now go. Let me get to know my niece before I have to leave for two weeks." He sits down on the arm of the chair. "I never thought I'd be pissed about going on tour, but I'm worried about leaving her."

"Don't be. I've got her. Take your shot, Jack Madden. Show the whole damn world how incredible Six Day War is. But promise me I get a private preview of your set with the whole band before you leave. I need to meet your new singer." Emerson told me she loved the singer they found after I left, and I've been dying to hear them since. "Want me to bring you back anything?"

"Nope. I'm good. Thanks." He doesn't take his eyes off the sleeping baby, and I don't blame him. She's everything.

The hum of the hospital relaxes me as I walk through the maze of corridors in search of the cafeteria. Following a sign, I turn down a hall and see Jessie coming toward me in pink scrubs and matching Crocs. She squeals.

"Well? Did she have the baby? I've been stuck in surgery all night and haven't had the chance to check in." She grabs both my hands, and I wince.

"She did. A baby girl named Elodie Madden-Alexander."

Her face softens. "Linc would have loved that."

"Yeah. I think he would have. Em's sleeping, but Jack's up there with her now, if you want to stop in."

"Thanks. Did you see the guys? They were here for a few hours, but Ford texted they were going home around two a.m. We'll have to let them know she had the baby." Jessie claps her hands with excitement, and I yawn in contrast.

"Let me get some caffeine before you make me deal with anyone else, okay?" My stomach growls as if on command, and Jessie laughs at me.

"Get a muffin too. They're delicious." She hugs me to her. "I'll talk to you later. Text if you need anything." She walks away, and I'm left wondering where the heck she gets her endless energy from, as I step into the cafeteria.

After grabbing a tea and a blueberry muffin the size of my head, I sit at a table and pull my phone out to check my messages.

One from Daphne, two from Chloe, and one from Mom.

Everyone wants to know if I'm okay after the funeral.

At least I can give them some happy news this morning.

I'm sending them all a picture of Elodie when the chair next to me is pulled out. My head snaps up, thinking it's Jack or Theo, but I'm surprised to see Axel sitting down instead.

"How ya doin, baby momma?" His black ball cap is pulled low over tired eyes as he wraps an arm around my shoulders and tugs me to him.

"Axel." I hug him back. "We missed you yesterday. What are you doing here? I thought Jessie said the guys went home."

"Yeah. They did. I talked to them this morning though. I just got in yesterday and missed the service. But I thought I'd check in. Are you back in town permanently? Did you and Sinclair figure your shit out? You know I'm always an option, right?"

I laugh him off. "Yeah. I know, and thank you for that. But you know Cooper has my heart. Even if we've still got a few things to talk about." Just saying it out loud hurts, though, in a way I'm not sure will ever go away.

"You guys gonna talk soon?" Axe seems pushier than usual, but I'm so freaking tired, maybe it's just me.

"I'm not sure, Axe. He's still pretty mad."

Axel's hand, which had been resting on the back of my chair, begins playing with my hair, making me a little uncomfortable. "Do me a favor, baby momma. Can you tell Sinclair he's got something of mine, and I want it back?" He tugs on my hair, pulling a little too hard on my scalp.

"I was never yours, Axe." I try to laugh his innuendo off.

Axel lets go of my hair and taps the table with his hand. "Just tell him for me, okay?" He stands up and stares at me, waiting for an answer.

"Sure." I hesitate at the uncomfortable vibes rolling off him. "I'll tell him."

"We could have been good together, Carys."

Something about the look in his eyes puts me on edge, but I try to shake it off. I just need sleep. "Whatever you say, Axe."

He laughs, then picks up my muffin and walks away.

That could possibly go down as my strangest conversation with Axel since I've known him. And I've had some strange ones during that time. Maybe we all need a little bit of sleep.

COOPER

"Do you think your brothers will be able to crack the flash drive?" Ford asks Rook as the three of us walk back into the hospital for the second time in twelve hours.

Rook glares back at Ford, annoyed. "Do you think I'd waste my time driving two hours if I didn't think they could do something?"

"We should have known it would be encrypted. Axe isn't stupid," I groan, frustrated that we're stuck until someone can get access to the drive. "He was always good with the tech stuff."

"He knows how we operate, Sinclair. Nothing about this will be easy." Ford's entire demeanor changes as Jessie strolls into the lobby of the hospital, looking like unicorn glitter is about to explode from her body.

She jumps into Ford's arms with a smile plastered to her face.

I look away while they kiss like they haven't seen each other in months instead of hours.

"You guys should head up now. Jack and Theo just left, so it's not too crowded." She smacks Ford's ass, and her smile grows. "And you should be quick about it, because I have another twelve-hour shift tonight. And once I crash, there'll be no waking me up until I need to shower and get back here."

Ford wraps his arms around her waist. "Oh, I can be quick."

Rook coughs into his fist. "Not something to be proud of, brother."

"Jealous, Rook?" Jessie counters before bouncing on her toes and kissing Rook and me both on our cheeks. "See you boys later."

I watch her leave, then look at Ford. "Well, Jessie's certainly in a great mood."

"We haven't wanted to say anything because it's so early, but she's pregnant. Today's the first day of her second trimester. According to the doctor, the chances of complications go way down once you're past the first twelve weeks. Add that to the fact she probably just held a brand-new baby, and yeah, Jessie's on cloud nine." Ford shoves his hands in his pockets like he's embarrassed to be happy with everything else going on.

I clap him on the back. "Congrats, man. That's amazing."

"That's one lucky kid," Rook tells him. Then he adds, "Better you than me."

We sign in with the front desk and get our badges. "Room 309, gentlemen. There's already a visitor there. And one visitor at a time." The woman behind the desk glares at us over her glasses.

"Ladies first, Sinclair." Rook motions for me to go ahead, and I punch him in the shoulder.

"Even with a bullet wound, I'll still kick your ass in a race."

"True story." Ford drops into one of the old vinyl chairs in the waiting room, and I ignore them as they fight over whether I could win.

Rook's slow as shit, so I'd definitely win.

When I find room 309, the door is cracked open, so I knock quietly before walking in. What I see is a sucker punch to the gut. Carys is curled up in a recliner, wearing a tank top and sweatpants, with a tiny little baby lying against her chest in nothing but a diaper and a big pink bow. My heart screams *mine*, while my brain screams *run*.

Her eyes are closed, and she's humming a soft song while both the baby and Emerson sleep.

When I close the door behind me, Carys's eyes slowly open, and a tender smile spreads across her gorgeous face. Every ounce of hurt I hold over this woman washes away in an instant, and I want nothing more than to wrap her in my arms. But that can't happen now.

"Hey," she whispers.

I take a step closer and stare in wonder at the tiny baby. "Hey. How are you doing?" I ask just as quietly.

"Well," she whispers, smiling, and my entire body relaxes. "I'm not the one who gave birth, so I'm doing pretty well. A little tired." She shrugs. "And my hand may never quite heal from the insane hold Em had on it last night, but . . ." She angles herself to give me a better view of the sleeping baby. "Little Miss Elodie was worth it."

"She's beautiful." I trace a finger gently along her tiny arm, and her fingers spread wide open, startled. "She looks like Linc," I whisper in awe.

"Wait until she opens her eyes. They're all Emerson. But everything else is all her daddy." Sadness creeps into her voice as she adjusts Elodie and stands from the chair. "Do you want to hold her?"

I shake my head. "I don't want to break her."

Carys laughs at me. "You won't break her, Coop. Sit down, and I'll lay her in your arms."

I hesitate for a moment before sitting down and then hold still as Carys carefully transfers a sleeping Elodie into my arms. The baby roots around for a minute until she gets comfortable, then yawns so big, I half expect her jaw to come unhinged. Her warm skin is soft under my hand,

and for a moment, I forget about the shitstorm currently surrounding us.

Forget that I'm furious with the woman in front of me.

Forget that Linc isn't about to walk through that door and hold his daughter.

But that peace is short-lived.

Carys takes a step back and covers her mouth with her hands. "You look really good holding a baby, Cooper." Pain laces her voice, and the vise around my heart tightens.

"I never cared about that, Carys. We could have adopted. We could have fostered. We could have used a surrogate." She closes her eyes, but I don't stop, making sure to keep my voice calm and quiet so I don't wake Elodie or Emerson. "We could have had as many years together as we wanted before we had to figure it out. But we would have figured it out together because I loved you."

She gasps just as I realize what I said.

"Loved." She holds my eyes as tears well in hers. "Past tense."

"We can't do this here, Carys. It's not the—"

"No," she cuts me off. "You wouldn't talk to me at the hospital. You wouldn't even look at me yesterday. Don't tell me now's not the time, unless you're ready to tell me when that time will be. I need to talk to you, Cooper. I still love you. I always have, and I always will. I shouldn't have taken away your choice when I did. I was so wrong to end things. You have to believe me."

Her words loosen the tightness I've been holding onto for a month, but there's nothing I can do about them now. "Believing you isn't the issue, Carys. Trusting you . . . That's a different story." Saying the words feels wrong, but if I want to keep her safe, I need to keep her at a distance while we figure this shit out.

Carys flinches and steps back as if I physically hurt her.

She runs her hands through her hair and turns away for a moment. When she turns back, a determined glint dances in her green eyes. "You can be as angry as you want, Cooper Sinclair, but I love you, and I know you love me too. So be pissed. Be hurt. Be as mean to me as you want. I'm not going anywhere this time. I'm not making that mistake again."

The spark I love in this woman is firing in a million vibrant colors as she fights for us.

I just wish she'd have done it sooner.

Carefully, I stand with Elodie in my arms, then look down at the little plastic baby bed on wheels. How the fuck are you supposed to put a baby down to sleep in something that moves?

Carys takes pity on me and gently lays Elodie down in the bed, then stands in front of the door. "I'm going to be here for another month, and we're going to talk before I leave, Coop. I refuse to accept that we're over. I'm not letting you throw us away, like I did."

I reach around her to grab the doorknob, and she moves to the side.

I take one step through the door before she stops me again. "Oh . . . Axe wanted me to tell you that you've got something of his, and he wants it back. He was being weird about it. I kinda thought he was talking about me."

An eerie chill settles against my skin as I turn around slowly. "When did you see Axel?"

"He sat with me this morning while I was having tea in the cafeteria. He was acting strange, but it's Axe. He owes me a blueberry muffin." She crosses her arms over her chest and leans against the doorframe.

I run a hand gently over the back of her hair, without any thought to the possessive move as I work through a million different scenarios at once, drawing on every ounce of training I've ever had. "Carys . . . baby, I need you to tell me exactly what he said."

Her eyes grow wide with confusion. "Coop, what's going on?"

"I can't explain everything right now, but I need you to tell me exactly what he said." I wrap my hand around the back of her neck, desperate to get her the hell out of here.

"Umm . . . He called me baby momma, asked if you and I were back together yet, and said something about how him and I could have been good together. Then he told me to tell you that you had something of his and he wanted it back. Like I said, I thought it was a joke and that he meant me."

"Shit." I drop my hand and take a step back. "I have to find the guys. Do not leave this room unless one of us is with you. Understand?"

Carys wraps trembling arms around herself. "You're scaring me."

"Good. Then you know I'm serious. If you see Axel, I need you to call me, then call security. Understand?" I can't believe this motherfucker followed us back here and was able to get so close to her.

Carys nods in agreement, and I rush down to the waiting room to find the guys standing across the room. "We've got a problem."

"What?" Ford steps forward.

"Axel was here." My blood rages when I think about him near her. "He approached Carys in the cafeteria and told her I had something of his."

"Fuck," Rook grunts.

Ford pulls out his phone and steps away while he warns Jessie. Once he shoves it back in his pocket, he looks between Rook and me. "So which one of you wants to move in with the girls?"

"Like I'm gonna leave her fucking side," I growl, ready to flay Axel alive for going near Carys.

"I'll help too, man. You can't cover everything twenty-four seven," Rook offers. "And the old man has to keep Jessie safe."

"Rook, get that flash drive to your brother. Go now. We need to know what's on it." Ford clasps my shoulder. "You glue your ass to Emerson and Carys until we know what the fuck's going on."

Like I'd trust anyone else with her life.

CARYS

"Go home, Carys. You look like hell." Jessie carefully picks Elodie up from the bassinet and coos before she moves to Emerson's bed, where she's lying on her side, awake but not paying any attention to us. "You're missing bonding time, Em. How about you sit up and hold her?"

"I'm tired," Em moans.

I could have told her that wasn't going to work.

I've tried, and that's as much as she's said all day.

But Jessie plays dirty. "Sit up, Emerson." Her tone is sharp, leaving no room for argument.

Em's eyes flash to Jessie. "It hurts, Jess." The agony in her voice conveys so much more than physical pain, so I instinctively sit next to her, on the opposite side of Jessie, and push the button to move the bed up. Trying to give her support in any way I can.

Jessie sways from side to side with Elodie as she begins rooting around, looking for something to eat. "Emerson Madden-Alexander, we love you and this beautiful little girl. And we all loved Linc. Do you think this is what he'd want? Would he want you to be so heartbroken that you ignored the last piece of him in this world? Because I don't think he would."

Emerson's big blue eyes fill as her lips tremble. "He's supposed to be here," she cries. "He wanted the baby. He wanted to get married. He loved me more than anything in this world . . . and I . . ."

Sobs wrack her chest as I gather her in my arms. "And now, *she* needs you more than anything in this world, Em. I know it hurts. But none of us can control that. What you can control is what you do now."

Tears soak my skin as she lets it out and hopefully lets go of some of her pain. "I think I need help," she whispers.

Jessie sits down on the other side of her, with Elodie getting fussier by the minute. "We'll be right here, Em. I've asked your doctor to come in and talk to you about options too. There's no shame in needing help, short- or long-term, and there are tons of medications out there that are safe for you and her."

Em nods her head. "Okay."

Jessie lays Elodie against Em's chest without giving her the option to say no, then grabs a bottle of formula and hands it to her. "You need to bond with your beautiful baby girl, Em." Jess sits down in the reclining chair and kicks her feet up on the bed. "I've got an hour before my shift starts, and I'm not going anywhere until your doctor comes in, okay?"

Emerson gently runs the nipple along Elodie's little lips until she latches on and snuggles in against her momma. "Yeah. Okay." She bites down on her bottom lip to stop the trembling. "I love you both so much."

"We love you too, Em. And we're not going anywhere." I lean back against the bed and kick my legs up next to hers.

"Yes." She turns her head toward me and sniffs. "You are. You need to go home and shower and sleep. I get out of here tomorrow, and I'll need help."

"Anything, Em. I'll do anything you need." I kiss the top of her head, then the top of Elodie's. I grab the hoodie Jack left for me earlier and throw it on over my tank. It smells like his expensive cologne, but it'll do. I pull my hair out of the hoodie, then mouth *thank you* to Jessie before slipping through the door, utterly exhausted, and hoping an Uber is close by.

"Carys," Cooper calls out my name, startling me. "You ready to go home?" He stands from a chair across the hall from Emerson's room and reaches for me.

I look around for the rest of the guys or something to explain what the hell he's doing here, but there's no one around except for a few nurses and some visitors in the hall. "Yeah, I'm going home." He's in the same clothes he was wearing earlier, but there's an unease to his face that's new. "Have you been here all day, Coop?"

He scans the hall without answering, then takes my hand in his. "Come on, let's get out of here."

It's the second time he's touched me today, and like he's electrically charged, the hairs on my arms stand on end at the connection. My body has always reacted to his this way, and I want to weep with relief over the fact that he's standing here in front of me. Instead, I throw my arms around him and hope to God he doesn't push me away. "Thank you for being okay, Cooper. My heart broke when I heard what happened to Linc, and admitting this probably makes me a horrible person, but all I could think was thank God it wasn't you."

Coop's body stiffens against mine before he pulls himself away. "We've got to get moving, Carys." His long legs eat up the distance as he practically drags me down the hall.

I struggle to keep up with him. "Hey." I tug back, a little embarrassed over my mini-meltdown and more than a little annoyed at his lack of response. "I get it. You're in a rush, but my legs are half the length of yours, and I haven't slept in over thirty-six hours, Cooper. Can you please slow down and tell me what the hell is going on?"

He speeds up instead of slowing down and slides us

both into an empty elevator before the doors close. Coop drops my hand and hits the emergency stop button, jerking it to a halt before his big body crowds mine against the wall. "I'm trying to protect you, Carys. You need to understand that Axel is dangerous." His warm breath ghosts over my face as every frightening word leaves his lips, chilling me to the bone. "If I thought you'd be safer, I'd send you back to Kroydon Hills, but you're better off here, where I can protect you." He bends his knees so our eyes are level. "Do you understand what I'm saying?"

"Not exactly." I gasp as my body shakes violently. "Dangerous how?"

Coop slams his hand against the wall of the elevator next to my head, and I turn my face away from his as a tear runs down my cheek. He hits the button again, and the elevator jerks back into motion before he wraps an arm around me and tucks me against him. "I can't answer that. But I need you safe." He ushers me through the doors the second they open and out into the parking garage.

"Coop . . ."

He doesn't stop to answer me. Instead, he just rushes us to his Jeep, shoves me in it, slams the door shut, and then moves quickly around to his side. Once we're both inside, Cooper turns his head and looks me over briefly with something unreadable in his eyes. "Buckle up."

He doesn't say anything else until we're on the interstate. "You were my first thought when I woke up in the hospital. My brain is still a little foggy on everything that led up to that point, but you were my first thought when I woke up." His words are spoken softly but with a force powerful enough to steal the breath from my lungs. He doesn't offer me anything more, and I take a few minutes before I ask any questions, scared to break whatever peace offering he's giving me, no matter how short or long it lasts.

"How are you doing now? How is your head and your . . . your—"

"My bullet wound?" he fills in. "The doc took the stitches out before I left Germany. Now it's just tape that will fall off soon." He looks at me out of the corner of his eye. "My memory still isn't completely back."

"Did Axel have something to do with what happened over there?" I can't believe I'm even asking the question and half expect him to say no. To tell me that sounds insane. Because it does. But Coop doesn't say any of those things.

"Yes."

One word. Three letters that just blew my mind.

"Oh, God," I gasp. "Who hurt you, Cooper? Who hurt Linc?" *Please let me be wrong.*

Cooper doesn't answer, but his knuckles tighten around the steering wheel, and I try to absorb what he's not saying. It doesn't make sense. None of it does.

Then I start thinking about the cafeteria earlier. Axel wasn't there to hurt me or anyone else. *Was he?* It's like a puzzle with pieces that don't fit together, but I try to make sense of it anyway.

"I don't understand . . . Why would Axe do this?" It's Axel. The goofball who's been joking around about marrying me for over a year.

"We're not sure. But our best guess is money. The problem is, we don't have any fucking clue what he's doing now, and the fact he came to you today can't be dismissed. But I promise you, I'll keep you safe. I'll be at the house with you and Emerson until this gets straightened out."

"Um, what?" I turn to look at him, not sure I heard him right. "What do you mean?"

"I'm staying with you guys until this is straightened out." Coop refuses to look at me as he turns onto our street, then parks in the driveway. "Give me your keys and let me clear the house before you come in."

I pull my keys from my bag and throw open the door. "No. I'm not letting you go in without me." He's out of his freaking mind if he thinks I'm going to sit out here like a good little girl and let him get hurt . . . again.

"Goddamnit, Carys." He slams the door shut behind him and catches up to me in two strides, grabbing my shoulder to stop me. "This isn't going to work if you don't listen to me."

"Oh, I'm going to listen to you." I wrench my arm away as a plan begins to form in my mind. "But you're going to listen to me too, Cooper Sinclair." I hand him my keys. "And either way, I'm going in that house with you."

Cooper groans. "Why do you insist on being such a pain in the ass?"

"Because you won't talk to me, but you think you have the right to tell me what to do. Well, guess what? Out of everything I've learned in the past year, the most important thing has been to stand up for myself and what I want." I walk ahead of him and wait at the front door. "I'm working on my communication skills, Coop."

He looks up to the sky as he groans, then unlocks the door, coming face-to-face with Jack and Theo.

They look between Coop and me and must sense the tension rolling off us in violent waves. "We're out." Theo salutes us.

"We're on our way to see Emerson." Jack basically ignores Cooper. "We should be back in a little while, and then, Brooklynn is coming over to run through the set one more time before we leave for the tour. You gonna be around, CC?"

"Yeah. I'll be here."

Jack tugs on the hoodie I'm wearing as I walk by him. "Am I getting that back before I leave?" His lips tip up in a crooked grin, and this fucker knows exactly what he's doing, which is taunting Coop, who storms away.

"I'll wash it tonight, you ass." I shake my head, and Jack's smile grows.

"You'll be thanking me later." He winks and closes the door behind him.

I lock it and watch Cooper drop a duffle bag, I hadn't even noticed he was carrying, next to the couch. He stretches his arms up over his head, exposing a strip of bare, golden skin above the waist of his jeans. My mouth waters.

God, I miss this man. But two can play at this game.

"Are you ready to talk?" I lift my eyes to his after staring for a moment too long, then slowly peel the hoodie off, leaving me in a thin pink tank that's pulled low in the front, exposing the tops of my breasts.

Cooper's already moved to the glass doors leading to the back yard and is checking the lock, when he turns around and audibly swallows, shaking his head. "No. I'm going to check the locks, then crash on the couch for a little while too." He lowers the blinds on the glass doors, then follows me up the stairs.

Heat colors my cheeks as exhaustion mixes with grief, frustration, and fear.

He might not forgive me yet . . . but I think he still wants me.

I know he still loves me.

And while nothing about this situation is good, if he's going to be here, in this house and in my space, I'm going to get this man to talk to me if it's the last damn thing I do.

Coop stops in Emerson's room, while I move into mine,

leaving the door open while I strip out of my sweats. Standing in my tank and black panties, I pull the blanket back on my bed as he walks into my room and forces his eyes from me while he checks the lock on my door. "Can I ask you something?"

Cooper turns around, with his eyes glued to my face like a perfect gentleman.

As if I don't know all the ways he can be ungentlemanly . . .

"Did you push me away at the hospital because you hate me?" There's a nervous quiver in my voice I wish I could hide, but I have to know. The thought has been playing over and over in my head since he admitted he thought of me when he woke up. "Or did you do it because you already knew about Axel and thought I was in danger?"

Cooper's eyes hold me hostage until he abruptly storms out of the room.

And somehow, for some reason, I think that might count as a win.

COOPER

I HADN'T GIVEN CARYS ENOUGH CREDIT. I WASN'T EXPECTING her to put two and two together just yet, which was stupid because that girl should never be underestimated in any way. I'm not sure why I didn't just tell her the truth.

That's a lie.

If I tell her the truth about Germany, we're going to have to talk about everything . . . including my discharge. And that wound is still way too raw to pick at yet.

I also don't know if I'm ready to fight a fight on two fronts now.

As I lay on this couch, knowing she's upstairs alone in her bed, every muscle in my body revolts. I want to go back up there and show her all the ways she's mine. All the reasons she was wrong to give up on us. To give up on me. But I don't.

One thing at a time. And the bigger issue right now is Axel.

The front door opening has me jackknifing up from the couch, with my Glock in my hand, and coming face-to-face with a now-scared-shitless woman.

"Holy shit." She drops to the floor.

"What the fuck, Sinclair?" Jack storms in. "Why do you have a fucking gun in my house?" he roars.

I tuck the gun in the back of my jeans as Carys comes flying down the stairs.

I swear to God, this girl would run toward danger instead of away from it.

"Sorry." I put my hands in the air to show Jack they're empty, while Theo helps the small redhead up. She's shaking, and for a moment, I feel like a fucking dick.

That is until Carys stands next to me, and I get my first good look at her. She must have thrown the sweatshirt from earlier on before she ran down here. It grazes the tops of her bare thighs, swallowing her entirely.

And. It's. Jack's.

Fuck me, I can't help the possessive rage that fills me at seeing another man's shirt on her beautiful body.

I tamp down the raging energy that's ready to explode at seeing her nearly naked in another man's clothes and turn my glare to her. "Everything's fine." My eyes trail up her beautiful bare legs, not stopping until I get to her frightened face. "It's fine."

Theo escorts the little redhead to the basement as Jack moves across the room, big-dick energy in full force. Problem for him is I'm the bigger dick.

"What the fuck was that, Sinclair?" He crosses his arms over his chest, and I've got to give him credit because he's not backing down.

"We've got a problem, and I need to make sure it doesn't touch Carys." I leave the rest unsaid, and Jack stares hard until he turns toward her.

"Are you okay?" His voice softens as he runs his hands over her arms, and I want to rip them from his body and beat him to death with them.

She nods. "Nothing for you to worry about. I'm going

to throw some clothes on and then come down to the studio. You owe me a preview of your set, remember?" Her smile is forced until she grabs my hand and squeezes. "I'll be back in a minute."

When she's out of sight, Jack drops his arms and moves into the kitchen. He pulls two beers from the fridge and offers me one.

"No thanks." I don't tell him my head's still fucked up from the concussion, and the last thing I need is to make it worse.

"Want to tell me what's going on and why you have a gun in my house? Is my sister in danger?" He glares, but I get it. I'd kill someone if they threatened Nattie.

"I don't know. Some stuff went down on our last op, and the team is going to be all over Emerson and Carys until we figure it out." It's the best I can do with what I can tell him.

"Do I need to cancel the band's tour? We're gone for two weeks."

"No. You're better off out of here and away from this shit. It's less for us to worry about and keep our eyes open for. It lets us focus on keeping the girls safe while this shit gets handled. Doesn't split focus by having more people in the house." The more people here, the bigger the chance of mistakes and the higher the risk to everyone.

"I don't like this, Sinclair." Jack pushes his hand through his hair as he blows out a frustrated breath. "This is my sister. I think I should take her somewhere else. Somewhere safe."

"You can't bring a new baby on tour with you, Jack. And she's going to be safer here with Rook, Ford, and me looking after her than she would be anywhere you can take her. I can't tell you more than that. But know that Linc was my brother. And that makes Emerson and Elodie family.

I'd fucking die before I let anything happen to them." I make sure he's getting what I'm saying because I mean every word. "We all would."

"I swear to fucking God, Sinclair, if anything . . . *anything* happens to them, I'll kill you myself."

I choose not to tell him that I'd like to see him try.

"Go on your tour, Jack. This'll all be over by the time you get back." *I hope.*

Jack considers my words for a minute. "You know she only has my hoodie because when we got to the hospital, she was cold, right?"

I laugh silently. "Yeah. I figured. Why? You gonna give me advice on Carys now?"

"Nah. Just a friendly reminder that, that girl upstairs is incredible. She broke down and told me what was going on when she flew back here last week. She loves you, not that I have any fucking idea why." He smiles like the creepy clown from *It*. "My sister's shattered right now because she can't fix what's broken. Don't do that to Carys." He grabs his beer and heads downstairs to the studio, leaving me behind to wonder if the pretty-boy rockstar isn't as dumb as I thought he was.

CARYS

I CONSIDERED LEAVING JACK'S HOODIE ON FOR A HOT minute, just to rile Cooper up, before deciding there are better, more mature ways of doing that. But I do need to break Coop's resolve and get him to talk to me somehow. The man has the self-control of a saint, but whether he wants to admit it or not, he has a possessive streak a mile wide.

Lucky for him, I happen to like it. Because the enraged look in his eyes when I came down in Jack's sweatshirt would have been as hot as the nine circles of hell if he was willing to admit a fire is still burning between us. I know it's there. I can taste it.

I just need to fan those flames higher and remind him.

Drastic times call for drastic measures.

I slide a pair of gray booty shorts up my legs and a soft blue flannel I stole from Cooper's room last year over my tank. A little plumping of the boobs—because let's face it, without a bra pushing them up, they're not too much to look at—and a quick flip of my hair, and I march out of my room and down the stairs to find Coop standing alone in the kitchen.

He's leaning against the counter. Dark jeans hang from his lean hips, and his bare feet are crossed at the ankles. The muscles in his chest are stretching his white tee to the limits as his thumbs fly across the screen of his phone.

He looks absolutely exhausted.

And if I'm honest with myself, he looks like he's absolutely *mine*.

He looks up quickly as I enter the room, and I catch a smile before he manages to mask it. "Nice shirt."

"It was better when it smelled like you." I stand across from him and mirror his stance, deciding bold is the way to go. We've never been about games, and I'm not about to start now. "Are the guys downstairs?"

"Yeah. They went down with the redhead I scared shitless." He shrugs, like she should have been prepared for a gun to be waved in her face, and finishes whatever text he was sending without looking back up.

I toe his bare foot with mine. "Any word from Rook?"

"Yeah. No answers yet though. We need to stay put for now." He shoves his phone in his back pocket and straightens.

"Cooper . . ." I push off the island and place a foot between his, trying to crowd him the way he likes to crowd me, and bring my body close enough to feel the heat coming off him. I push just a little further and lift my hand to his chest but get stopped by Theo before I can make contact.

"Come on, guys. We're ready to start." He grabs a few bottles of water from the fridge and hurries back to the basement studio, leaving us behind.

I tug on Cooper's hand, and electricity races to life between us. "Come on," I tease. "They're about to start."

"You go. I'm staying up here. I have a few calls to make."

I spin on him and glare. "You're not going to make this easy, are you?"

Cooper drops his head back and stares at the ceiling for a beat before bringing his eyes to me. "Nothing about us was ever easy, was it?" His tone is lethal. It's unforgiving and sounds nothing like Cooper, but I stand my ground.

"That's where you're wrong, Coop. You and me . . ." I take a chance and place my hands on his chest as I step into him. Just a breath separates us as Cooper stands rigid. "Loving you was the easiest thing I've ever done in my life. It was everything else that got in the way because I let it. But I'm not going to make that mistake twice."

My fingers flex against his chest, sizzling from the close contact. But I force myself to take a step back. Then another. "I'm going downstairs."

I turn away from him and take a few steps before stopping and tilting my head. "If that sounded familiar, it's because you said it to me once, and I never forgot it. And I'd bet my life neither did you."

With that, I skip down the steps to the studio in the basement, giving Cooper some time to think about what I just said. Hoping this man can forgive me because I don't know if I'll ever be able to forgive myself if he doesn't.

When I get down there, the guys have already set up, and Jack's tuning his favorite guitar. "No Lucas tonight?"

Theo rips his Nirvana tee off, then spins his drumstick through his fingers and laughs. "Nope. Stone's hooking us up with a new bassist. We're meeting him tomorrow. Lucas didn't want to drop out of school halfway through the semester."

"You ready, Brooklynn?" Jack looks at the petite redhead with a concerned look in his eyes.

She adjusts her mic. "Are there going to be any more guns waved in my face tonight?" Her voice is timid and quiet, and her posture is closed in, like she hates the idea of being the center of attention. Not what you typically see in a singer.

"Sorry about that." I flinch. Not exactly the best first impression.

"Count us off, Theo." Jack nods his head as Theo counts them down, and a familiar chord echoes around the room.

"Holy shit. You finished the song," I exclaim. It's the song he spent last spring working on. My body thrums with excitement before Brooklynn even sings the first note. But then she does, and everything stops. I never would have expected the voice that comes out of this woman. She's a fucking powerhouse. Flawless.

All the noise of the past few weeks quiets, and I get lost in the music with chills covering my body.

He did it.

Jack finished the song, and it's the best he's ever written.

I know, without a doubt, they're never coming back here because this is the break they've been busting their asses for. One song rolls into another, and before I know it, they've finished the set, and I've jumped to my feet. "Guys." I hug Jack, holding him tight. "That was perfect."

Theo piles on the two of us, turning me into a Six Day War sandwich. "I love you guys."

"Thanks for helping us get here, CC." Jack kisses the top of my head before pulling away and going over a few things with Brooklynn.

"You could come with us, you know?" Theo ducks his head as if he can't believe what he's saying.

"I *would* make a great groupie, but you know I can't." I lift up on my toes and kiss his cheek. "But I promise to be your number-one fan, no matter where I am."

There's no longing.

No regret.

I'm so damn happy for them, but that's not where I'm meant to be.

It never was.

COOPER

"WHAT THE FUCK DO YOU MEAN HE CAN'T CRACK THE code?" I clench my jaw so hard, I'm surprised my teeth don't crack as the throbbing behind my eyes intensifies.

Rook groans on the other end of the call. "It's not an instant thing, Sinclair. I'm not saying he won't get it, just that he hasn't gotten it *yet*. I'm heading back to San Diego first thing in the morning, and Ash is going to keep working on it for us. He said he's got someone he can ask for help. But it's gonna take some time."

"I gotcha." I walk the perimeter of the house, making sure there aren't any issues since I'm already out here. "Try to get some sleep, okay?"

Rook is a notorious insomniac. The fucker can go days without sleeping. "Sure, *Mom*. I'll get right on that. I don't have anybody warming my bed, like some of us do."

"Whatever. Ford is the only one of us with someone warming his bed, asshole." Nothing seems out of place outside. Two shitheads are getting high on the beach, judging by the smell, but that's about it.

"That's your own fault, brother. She apologized. What more do you want? You want her to grovel?" He hums. "That's not a bad idea. I have zero doubt that Carys looks incredible down on her knees."

My already fucked up vision goes red with rage. "Get that picture out of your head, motherfucker."

He laughs like the sadistic bastard he is. "Yeah. That's

what I thought. Keeping her out of this in Germany was a solid plan. But she's in it now. I mean, you're living with her. Doesn't get much more *in it* than that."

"Ya think?" I hate when Rook is right. And the asshole is almost always right.

He's the best analytical thinker on the team. He can remove his emotions and opinions from nearly any situation and give the unbiased advice we need. Helpful but really fucking annoying when he's telling you what to do with your own life. "Call me when you get back tomorrow."

"Yeah. Try not to screw it up before I get there." He ends the call, and I walk into the backyard, cursing as I turn the corner a little too close to the house and catch a branch to the face from the oversized shrub.

"Shit." I press down against the spot on my cheek and come away with blood on my finger.

"You okay?" Carys's voice carries down from her balcony.

"I'm fine. How long have you been out there?" *How much did you hear* is what I really want to ask but don't.

"I just came out a few minutes ago. I couldn't sleep." She stands with her hands resting on the wrought-iron railing in nothing but an oversized sleep shirt hanging off one shoulder. It skims the very tops of her thighs, and my cock jerks in my jeans as it takes notice.

Hell, my whole fucking body jumps to attention with awareness.

"Go inside and lock your damn door, Carys." My words come out harsher than I meant for them to, but I swear to God, it's like she's trying to put herself at risk.

I step through the glass doors and lock them behind me as Carys storms down the stairs, looking like a pissed-off goddess. Her green eyes flare as she gets in my face.

"You know." She points her finger at me, poking my chest. "I love bossy Coop, but only when there's a damn orgasm promised at the end of it. So, unless you're planning on making me come, you need to back off and keep your commands to yourself."

Her face is flushed and gorgeous as her chest heaves with each hitch of her breath, and I have to fist my hands to keep myself from touching her.

From taking.

But Carys has other ideas.

She takes a step forward and crashes her lips to mine in a furious kiss.

We're all teeth and tongues as need and anger war with each other.

I want this woman more than I've ever wanted anything in my life.

I grab both of her wrists in my hands and slam her back against the wall. Gathering her wrists in one hand, I hold them tight above her head and skim my fingers along the bare skin of her soft thigh.

Carys whimpers as her pupils blow wide with need.

"Is this what you want?" I ask with a vicious growl as I skim my teeth over the exposed skin of her shoulder. Not thinking straight. Lust and anger fueling me.

She rolls her hips against mine in response, and blood roars in my ears.

"You wanna ride my cock?"

Carys pulls against the tight grip I've got on her and turns her head, trying to capture my lips, but I let go of her wrists and drop to my knees.

"Cooper . . ." Her nails bite against my skin as she grabs my shoulders for purchase.

The pain feels too fucking good, compared to the numbness I've had since waking up in Germany. "If you're a good girl, instead of a fucking tease, maybe I'll let you come before I lock you in your goddamned room."

I run my tongue up the inside of her smooth thigh, then nuzzle my nose along the damp seam of her silk panties, inhaling her scent. She's warm and wet and smells fucking fantastic. But she backs her hips away from my face and yanks on my hair, tilting my head up. Forcing me to look at her. "What's wrong? You wanted to come, didn't you?" My raging hard-on strains against the zipper of my jeans, but the hurt look on her beautiful face has my heart sinking and my cock deflating.

"Stop." The word comes out shaky as she takes a step away and rubs her wrists where red marks are forming from the way I held her. "This isn't you, Cooper. You're not cruel."

"Carys . . ." I'm not sure what I'm planning to say or what there even *is* to say. I never meant to be cruel, no matter how angry I am. Not with her. Never with her.

"No. I'm not going to let you do this to us, Coop. This hot-and-cold thing. One minute, you're furious at me, and the next, you're in a pissing contest with Jack because I'm wearing his damn sweatshirt." She crosses her arms under her chest, plumping up her breasts, and even a case of blue balls mixed with regret can't stop my mouth from watering.

"Eyes up here, asshole." Carys shoves my shoulder, and I stand back up and adjust my dick like the prick I've become.

"I'm pissed, Carys. Not dead." Frustration simmers because I know she's right. I've been all over the place since I got back from Germany, and she's taken the brunt of my anger. Heat burns my side from the way I twisted, irritating my healing incision, and I grunt and grip my side.

Accusing eyes watch my movements carefully before her face softens. "Talk to me, Cooper. You haven't even told me what the doctor said or when you have to report back for duty."

She's pushing for answers I'm not sure I'm ready to give. I haven't even come to terms with the extent of my injuries and what that means for my life yet. How am I supposed to talk about it with her?

Carys moves into the kitchen and fills the kettle, then goes about making us each a cup of tea. Once she's handed me one, she blows on hers and looks at me over the top of the mug as we stand on opposite sides of the island. "Well . . . ?" Green eyes attempt to stare into my soul. "What did the doctor say?"

I watch the steam billow from the top of her tea and groan, trying to buy myself time. "I don't know how to do this, Carys." It's the most honest thing I can tell her.

She places her mug on the marble and waits. "How to do what, Cooper? We were always friends."

"We were never fucking friends," I roar. "You were the love of my life."

I flash back to the day after Nattie's wedding . . . To the pain of watching her walk away on that goddamned beach.

I knew when I woke up next to her that morning, she was going to do it.

I didn't want to accept it, but I knew it was coming.

The night before hadn't been us coming back together, it was her saying goodbye with every touch. Every whispered word. But none of that prepared me for the pain of watching her walk away and not being able to stop it. "I got down on my knees and begged you not to destroy us. But you don't seem to remember that."

The pounding in my head grows stronger. "I got hurt, and all of a sudden, everything was better for you."

I study her face. Black bags line her tired eyes.

She's exhausted, and I'm being a dick, but I can't stop now. "Why is that, Carys? Explain to me how my getting hurt fixed all our issues in your mind. Because it didn't fix a damn thing for me. It fucked everything up even more."

She gasps as if I slapped her.

"Leaving you on that beach was the most painful thing I thought I'd ever have to do. But I was wrong. Because every day after that, I had to wake up, knowing I was the reason we broke. And that pain grew each day. But I did it because I thought I was protecting you in the long run. I was okay with the pain because I was saving you from the hurt down the line."

Her hands shake and grip the edge of the counter. "Just because I'm not sick this week doesn't mean I won't be next week, Cooper. The rest of my life will be about managing my lupus, and I didn't want you to be stuck taking care of me."

When she looks up, it's with so much regret. "I knew . . ." She rubs her eyes and sighs. "I knew before you got hurt that I'd seriously fucked up. But I didn't know how to fix it. And then we got the call. And we thought—" A sob gets caught in her throat, but she doesn't cry. Instead, she walks slowly around the island until she's standing next to me. Her hands frame my face, and I close my eyes and let myself just feel her for a minute.

"I knew before you got hurt, Cooper. But when we got the call, it broke me. I didn't care who knew about us. All those months of being worried what everyone would think went flying out the window. I didn't care how pissed any of them were. And let me tell you, Nattie and Aiden were furious. None of it mattered. I promised myself I'd do whatever it took to earn your forgiveness."

This woman has no idea that I forgave her before I got

on the plane after my sister's wedding. That a part of me understood what she was trying to do. But a different part, a larger part, hasn't gotten past the hurt of her throwing us away so easily.

Her thumb traces the scratch on my cheek before working its way up to my temple. It feels so damn good, I'm not sure I can even speak, but I force myself to try.

"Forgiving is the easy part, Carys. You're forgiven. You did what you thought you needed to do. I forgive you."

She runs her fingers through my hair, soothing the ever-present throb behind my eyes. "Then why, Coop? Why are you treating me like this?"

I give in and rest my hands on her waist. "Like what? Like I'm pissed?"

Her lip trembles in response, and I feel like a dick as she nods her head.

"Because I *am* pissed. I'm fucking furious that you gave up on us. I'm mad you didn't trust me. I'm angry Linc's dead, and I can't believe Axel's a fucking traitor. And I can't believe—" I cut myself off and stare over her shoulder.

But she's not having it. Carys brings my face back to hers. "What? You can't believe *what?*" she pushes.

I drag in a deep breath and fist her shirt in my hands. "I can't believe I was discharged."

"What does that mean?" she asks, confused.

"When the building fell . . . my head . . ." I stand, needing space, but Carys doesn't budge. Her arms circle my waist as she lays her head over my heart.

I hesitate, then wrap my arms around her and lean my chin on the top of her hair. "It messed with my vision. And the Navy is strict with what's acceptable. I no longer fall inside those parameters. I can no longer be a SEAL."

And I'm not sure how long that's going to take to sink in.

CARYS

"OH MY GOD, COOPER." MY HEART BREAKS WIDE OPEN.

As long as I've known this man, being a SEAL has been his dream. I tighten my hold on him as I soak his shirt with my tears. "I'm so sorry."

His hand runs over my hair and down my back. "I'm alive. That's more than Linc got. I'm also walking, which is more than Trick can do right now." He stiffens. "Don't cry for me, Carys. I'll be fine. But I'm fucking angry."

I made it all worse, and I'm not sure if I can fix it.

But I refuse to stop trying.

"Cooper." I look up at him, and there's so much hurt staring back at me that I almost turn away . . . Almost. "Do you still love me?" The words come out careful and quiet. But I got them out, and that's what matters.

"Carys." His voice hangs heavy between us.

"It's a yes or no answer, Coop. Tell me . . . Do you love me? Because I never stopped loving you. I don't think I could if I tried." I run my hands up his side, but he winces, and I immediately pull back.

Shit. His incision.

"It's okay. It's just sore."

My fingers gently slide under his tee, pushing it up his hard body and then trace the outside of his bandage with a feather-soft touch. Careful not to get too close to the incision, I watch goosebumps breakout over his flesh at my touch.

"Come to bed with me, Cooper." He lifts his brow in question, so I add, "Just to sleep. I promise I won't try and take your virtue." I smile but continue running my fingertips along his hot skin, reveling in the connection between us, no matter how small.

Baby steps.

When he doesn't budge, I beg, "Please, Coop. Come to bed with me. We both need to sleep, and I'd feel safer with you next to me." *Okay*, so it may have been a shitty move to play that card, but I don't want this man, who's only a few days out of the hospital, sleeping on the damn couch. And selfishly, I want to spend the night feeling him breathe.

I take a few steps forward and tug him behind me.

Cooper hasn't answered me yet, but he follows behind until we get close to the couch. Then he pulls away, grabs his bag from the floor, and double-checks the locks.

I stand there, waiting, hopeful.

And when he comes back to me and presses his palm to the small of my back, the heat of his skin sears through my shirt, branding me in a way only he can.

We walk silently up the stairs, stopping when we pass Jack's open door.

"Jack said you could crash in his room while he's on tour, if you wanted to." I peer into Jack's room, wishing he hadn't made the offer, but he did.

Cooper urges me forward with his hand, and we walk into my room instead, closing the door behind us. He drops his bag on the chair in the corner and checks the lock on the balcony doors, then pulls the sheer curtains closed. "You've got to be more careful until we know what's going on, Carys. And being careful means you have to be vigilant."

He might not be able to tell me he loves me, but I know he does.

It's in his actions, even if it's not in his words.

"Sorry. I'll try." I hit the light switch, leaving the room bathed in the moonlight filtering in through the curtains, and climb into bed. I lie on my side, watching Coop strip down to his boxers and remove his shirt, and another silent tear trails down my cheek.

His beautiful body is a kaleidoscope of colors, with fading bruises, healing cuts, and scrapes he's quick to cover with a sheet once he slides into bed.

Instinctively, I reach out and trace the bruising over his chest, and Cooper stiffens momentarily. While I quietly hum what's become my favorite song since the first time I sang it to him in this bed, his body relaxes beside mine. I lay my head down on the pillow, facing him, instead of draping myself over him like I wish I could, and just look. This beautiful man, who's so strong and stubborn, has been through so much, and I can't help but wish I could take away the pain.

"Thanks for taking care of me, Cooper."

Coop lies on his back, staring at the ceiling. He doesn't say anything, so I wait.

After a while, I turn away from him and curl up, trying to take the win of him being here next to me, even if ignoring his silence is hard. He's here. That's enough.

I'm not sure how much time passes, but as I finally feel myself drifting off to sleep, I hear Cooper whisper, "I'll never stop loving you, Carys."

I'd planned on waking up early so I could get back to the hospital for Em, but setting an alarm must have slipped my mind last night. *Gee . . . I wonder why.*

What do they say about people who talk to themselves?

Oh right, it's only bad when you start answering.

Oops.

That was the best night's sleep I've had in months, and I have absolutely no doubt why. Even if the man himself is already up and out of bed.

I slide my hand across the cool sheets, wondering how long he's been awake and where he is. Just then, the door to my bathroom opens, and steam billows into the room, answering my question.

Cooper steps through next, with one of my pale-pink, fluffy towels wrapped around his waist. His hair is wet, and a single droplet travels down his muscular chest and over the indents of his abs like I wish I could do with my tongue.

Holy hell. When was the last time I had an orgasm?

Because I think I'm about to spontaneously combust.

"See something you like, Carys?"

I slowly drag my eyes back up his body and sit up. "Nope. Not really."

"Okay then." He grabs his boxers from his bag and pulls them up his legs, before letting the towel drop, then snaps the waistband against his skin. "You want to head to the hospital soon?"

I desperately want to kiss the smirk off his smug face but remind myself two can play this game. With a plan in place, I hop off the bed. "Yup. Just let me shower first." I turn my back to Cooper and pull my shirt over my head, leaving me clad in only my red-plaid cheeky panties. My hair hangs down, brushing against my shoulder blades as I turn just my head and toss him my shirt. It smacks him in the face and falls to the floor as he stands there, staring, while I walk into the bathroom.

A strangled groan sounds from the other side of the door as I close it.

I can't help but be the one smirking now.

I'd say that's one point to me.

COOPER

WELL, THAT FUCKING BACKFIRED.

I'm on edge, watching the curves of Carys's body before she disappears through the bathroom door. The dimples above her ass wink at me as she goes. *Damn*. She's the most gorgeous woman I've ever seen. She always will be.

When the door clicks shut behind her, I finish getting dressed and head for the kitchen, needing a jolt of caffeine and maybe another cold shower.

It's hard to believe we slept as late as we did.

It's almost noon, but I guess we needed it.

I know I did.

Why does everything look different after a solid night's sleep?

Once I figure out the fancy-ass coffee maker, I stand there, staring at it while it brews, as if I could make the damn thing work faster. This shiny silver equipment probably cost more than some people's car payments but was still grinding the coffee beans after what felt like a century passed.

I blame my twin sister for my coffee addiction.

I've just poured a cup when the front door opens, and Emerson walks through it, with Rook holding the baby in a car seat behind her. "Uh . . . hey guys. I didn't know you were coming home this morning."

Emerson doesn't say anything as she walks into the kitchen and grabs the coffee out of my hands before drinking half of it. "They don't let you sleep in that stupid place. Every time Elodie would sleep, a nurse would come in to check on me and wake her up. I can't take it anymore. I'm done. I need a gallon of coffee and forty-eight hours of sleep." She thinks about that for a second, then adds, "Maybe not in that order."

Then she walks away.

Specifically, up the damn stairs, while Rook and I stand in place, not sure what just happened.

As if on cue, the tiny little human in the carrier stretches small arms—covered in long white sleeves with pink polka dots and weird-looking little mitten things—over her head. She lets out a wail I wouldn't think could come out of something that small.

Rook drops the overnight bag from his shoulder to the floor and swings the carrier on top of the island between the two of us as we stare at the crying baby. She sounds like a baby dinosaur. And trust me, thanks to my sister-in-law's little brother, I know exactly what that sounds like.

Carys flies into the room. "What the hell is wrong with you two?" She unstraps Elodie from the torture device she's in and brings her up to her shoulder as she sways back and forth, shushing her gently. "Where's Emerson?"

I don't answer, so she turns to Rook. "Did you bring her home?"

With petrified eyes, he nods. "Yeah. She yelled at me to get her the hell out of the hospital." He shrugs his shoulder. "Not gonna lie. She scared me a little."

"Well, at least she was having some strong emotions. Yesterday, she was in a fog." Carys grabs the bag from the floor and shuffles through it, looking for something. "How was she? Other than wanting to leave? Did she show any interest in Elodie?"

She must find what she was looking for because she pulls a can of formula from the bag and smiles. "Jackpot."

"Emerson was changing the baby's diaper when I got there. She'd just signed her discharge papers." Rook eyes Elodie like a suicide bomber as Carys places her in his arms. "What the hell, Carys?"

"Support her head," she tells him as she adjusts his hold. "There you go." She turns back to the counter and grabs the formula. "She's hungry. Just give me a minute."

"Carys," Rook growls as Elodie's face turns into a tomato before she lets out a loud grunt, followed by a smell that could clear a football stadium.

Carys and I both take a step back, and Rook's eyes grow ten times in size. "Take her back. She exploded." And she did. Moisture is soaking through the polka dots on her back.

Carys giggles and takes a step back. "Come on, soldier boy. You can't handle a little baby poop?"

This shit's so funny, I don't bother correcting her, but Rook is losing his patience. "It's sailor, not soldier. And I don't clean up baby shit."

"Oh," Carys laughs harder. "And I should because I'm a girl?"

"Jesus Christ." Emerson storms down the steps, having changed into one of Linc's shirts and stretchy black pants. "Give me my daughter." She takes her from Rook's hands. "She's the size of one of your big, fat hands, Rook. Seriously." She rolls her eyes, then points to the bag. "CC, can you grab that bag?"

Carys nods, then her wide eyes dance between Rook and me as Emerson takes Elodie upstairs, mumbling about who's the bigger baby.

"Pretty sure she's talking about you, Rook." Carys pats

his chest before she darts up the stairs with the bottle and the bag.

Rook waits until both girls are out of sight before he steps behind the counter and washes his hands. "How can such a little body produce such a foul fucking smell?" He grabs a mug and fills it with coffee. "I've got news."

"Well, do you want to tell me what it is, or am I supposed to guess?"

He lays the flash drive on the counter. "The terrorist group Axel was working with . . . They didn't just kidnap those women. They're trafficking them. There's payment information, sale information. Spreadsheets full of names and wire information."

"What the fuck was Axe doing with it? Why would anyone give that kind of information to a Navy SEAL? Why did they trust him?" Why did *we* trust him?

"That's what we need to figure out, brother. I told Ford to meet us here later. He said he wanted to give Jessie some time to sleep before he came. He's scared to let her out of his sight. But we've got to figure out what we want to do with this information." He finishes his coffee, washes the mug, and places it on a towel next to the sink.

"What choice do we have? We've got to give whatever we find out over to the Navy." Axel's AWOL. What the hell else would we even do with it?

"Phoenix International specializes in putting an end to human trafficking." He lowers his voice, then crosses the room to go outside, and I follow. "They aren't constrained by the letter of the law the way you or I would be."

Fuck me.

I haven't told him yet.

Ford knows I was medically discharged. But I'd bet my last dollar, he'd shown me the respect to let me tell Rook myself. "Yeah, man. About that."

Rook turns around and crosses his arms over his chest. "Swear to God, Sinclair, if you're going to turn into some Pollyanna and try to tell me you won't even consider that there are other channels we should think about, I'm gonna lose my shit."

"That's not it." I run my hand through my hair, stalling. "Damn. This is hard."

"Spit it out," he snaps, getting annoyed. Probably thought I was going to say something shitty about the company his brothers built.

"I was medically discharged before I left Germany. I've already gone to base and filled out the final paperwork. The Navy's done with me." My head pounds, thinking about it. "Ten percent loss of vision." I shrug, trying to play down my despair. "Mine wasn't perfect to start with, so combined, it's too much for Uncle Sam."

"Fuucckk . . . Coop, man. That sucks. I can't believe . . . I'm sorry." Rook's searching for the right words, but there are none. Not for this. Not for guys like us.

"Yeah. So, I'm fine with handling this however we decide. I just want it handled. I want Axel to pay for everything he did." *For everything.*

"He will, brother. We'll make him pay." Rook throws an arm around me and pounds my back. "For Linc."

I agree, "For Linc."

CARYS

EMERSON IS STILL STRUGGLING, BUT SHE RECOGNIZES IT, which is a start. We got Elodie cleaned up and fed before I basically put both Em and her down for a nap. I'm about to sneak out of her bedroom when my phone vibrates in my pocket with an incoming call. Darting down the hall, I pull the phone out to see Aiden's name flashing across the screen and debate not answering just as the vibrating stops.

Okay. Guess that's that, then.

Until the vibrating starts again. Damnit. I slide my finger across the screen and lift it to my ear as I walk down the stairs. "Hey." *Because this isn't going to be awkward as hell.*

"Carys." His tone is clipped and quiet.

Two things my brother never is.

He's the talker in the bunch.

The one who's always laughing and loud.

"Listen, I'm going to be in town this weekend for a game Sunday night. I got permission from my Coach to see you Saturday." That's it. No *hi, how are you doing?* No *I'm sorry for being a jackass.* Just *I'll be in town.*

"Aiden . . . It's been a really long few days. The funeral was earlier in the week, and Emerson had the baby the next day. She just got home from the hospital. I don't know if I can meet you Saturday. And to be honest, I don't know if I have the energy to fight with you either." One of the things this whole mess has forced me to realize is that honesty may not always be the easiest thing, but I'm no longer filtering what parts of me my family gets.

This is me.

Take it or leave it.

"Care Bear, I'm playing a game thirty minutes from your house. I'm staying at a hotel fifteen minutes from you. At the very fucking least, let me come see you." He waits a moment, then adds, "Please."

"Wow. Sabrina really has you house-trained, huh? You just said please." It's a low blow, but I'm still mad at him.

"How about I bring dinner? It's got to be early though. I promised Coach I'd be back by eight." His voice sounds hopeful, and I should probably be grateful he's making an effort.

"Fine. Be here at four. And bring enough food for everyone." Cooper and Rook eye me as they come in from outside.

Coop silently asks who I'm talking to.

"Yeah, big brother." I watch a flash of annoyance cross Cooper's face. "Everyone. Emerson's home from the hospital with Elodie. And Cooper's staying here for a while—"

He cuts me off before I have a chance to finish. "Are you fucking kid—"

"Love you, Aiden," I singsong as I hang up.

This should be fun.

"Your brother's coming? Am I invited for dinner too?" Rook asks, a little too excited by the idea.

I stand from the bottom step I've been sitting on and run a hand down Cooper's chest, startling him. "You might not want to be here that night. Aiden was pretty pissed when I told everyone about us."

Rook grabs his keys from the counter and smiles.

"You've been shot. Shouldn't that be a *Get Out of Jail Free* card?"

I move to block Rook's path. "Excuse me, but am I the jail in this scenario?" He surprises me when he hugs me, his lips brushing the shell of my ear.

"Push him, Carys. He might not be ready to admit it yet, but he needs you." When he pulls away, there's a devious glint in his hazel eyes.

I catch my bottom lip between my teeth and nod. "I gotcha. Thanks, soldier."

Rook growls, "You do it just to piss me off, don't you? You've got to know the difference between a soldier and a sailor by now."

I laugh and walk into the kitchen as Cooper follows Rook to the door and locks it behind him.

"Are you hungry?" The fridge is full of leftovers from the reception after the funeral. "Bingo." I pull out a small tin of lasagna and pop it in the oven. "This should warm up in a few minutes."

"Thanks," Coop murmurs without looking up.

Great. We're back to one-word answers. "You know, I was joking earlier about you not being here when Aiden comes Saturday night, but it might actually be a good idea for you to let me deal with him first."

Cooper's face softens when he steps in front of me and tucks a lock of hair behind my ear, then wraps that same hand around my neck in a possessive move I know and love. "He was that bad in Kroydon Hills?"

I think back to that day.

To the fear and the pain.

To the silent deals I made with whatever god there was for me to beg.

Then I remember what it felt like to tell our family I was in love with this man and the horrible way my brother responded, and a chill runs down my spine. "Yeah, it was pretty awful and unlike Nattie, Aiden and I haven't spoken since."

"You and Nattie have talked it through though? I've texted her, but we haven't talked since the hospital."

"Oh, Cooper." I tip my head back to look at him. "You've got to talk to her. She's so worried about you."

"Tell me about it." His words are demanding as they dance across my skin. "Tell me what happened that day."

"You don't want to hear this, Coop." I trace my finger along the bruise under his eye that's almost completely faded away. "It was hell. We were all in hell." My thumb trails down his cheek, then over his bottom lip as the muscles in his throat tighten.

"No one knew about us, and at first, I couldn't have cared less. We were all a mess, so no one noticed I was catatonic except Chloe and Belles." I fight back the tears that well in my eyes as I'm drawn back to the worst day of my life.

"Then we got the call, and we found out you were alive, and I . . ." The words get caught in my throat as I try to choke down the emotions. "We all . . ." No words can adequately explain the pain I experienced after that.

I swallow down the anguish and force myself to keep going. "I needed Coach to let me go with him to Germany, so I had to tell them all. And honestly, by then, I'd have screamed it from the Empire State Building if it meant I got to see you." I picture my brother's reaction and cringe as the first tear falls. "Nattie and Aiden . . ."

Cooper takes pity on me and pulls me into his arms as I sob against his chest. "We thought you were dead, and then you weren't. I couldn't let Coach go to you alone. I needed to be there. I had to. For me, and I thought for you too. So I told them the truth." I curl my arms around his shoulders, holding him tight to me, feeling his heart beat against mine. "I told them I loved you and that I was going."

"How did they take it?" His words are soft. Concerned.

"I honestly thought Nattie was going to take a swing at me. But I ended up being the only one to hit anyone." I'd never done that before in my life.

Cooper pulls me back and frames my face. "Who'd you hit, baby?"

My entire body relaxes at his words.

When he's not actively trying to hate me, the love I know he still has for me slips out.

I wish I could physically wrap the words around me. "I slapped Aiden."

He doesn't speak. He just stares at me, then shifts his eyes to look out the window.

I feel like I'm losing him. Like we were making progress and it's slipping through my fingers. "We can fix this right now, Cooper. We can fix it all. Everything I broke can be fixed in a single breath." My lips brush gently over his before he backs away and rips his ringing phone from his pocket.

"Shit," he mutters, then looks from the phone to me. "I can't do this right now, Carys."

"What changed, Coop? What happened?" I'm desperate to know what I can do to fix it.

He looks at me with anguished eyes. "Everything," he tells me before heading outside and slamming the door shut behind him.

The thud of the heavy door echoes just as Elodie's cries carry down the stairs.

I feel you, sister. You and I are both going to have ourselves a good cry.

COOPER

Twintuition is real and alive between Nattie and me.

I'm reminded of this as I slam the back door closed behind me, then check to make sure the damn glass didn't shatter in the process. My sister has always had the worst timing imaginable. It isn't even worth ignoring her call because she'd just keep calling until I answered or turned my damn phone off. And the latter isn't an option.

"Hey, Nat." I walk the perimeter of the yard, not wanting to go far from the house.

"Two goddamned weeks, Coop," she yells. "I spent two weeks calling you, and when you finally answered your phone, you basically hung up on me before we even got to talk. What the *shit* is up with that?"

"What the shit?" That's a new one.

"Shut up. I'm pregnant with fucking twins and hormonal as hell, and you're scaring me to death, asshole. You said what . . . maybe two sentences to me when you talked to me the other day. Then I have to find out from Sabrina that you're having dinner with Murphy Saturday night, but you can't even be bothered to call your twin sister back." With every word, her voice becomes more shrill.

She blows out a breath and quietly adds, "We shared a womb, Cooper. You owe me."

"Are you done, Nat?" I manage to control my tone. So that's something, right?

She sniffs, and I feel like a giant dick. "Yes."

"I've been stateside for four days, and all hell has officially broken loose in that time. I'm sorry I haven't called. Things are a mess. I haven't talked to Declan either." I pull out a chair on the back deck near the door and get comfortable for a long fucking talk that I'm not altogether ready to have with my twin. "I'm okay, but things are complicated right now."

"Things like your relationship with our *stepsister*?" Of course, she fucking went there first.

I look out over the sand, as foamy white waves lap at the beach, trying to calm down while my blood pressure roars in my ears and I ready for war. "Yeah. Among other things, you could say *Carys* and I are complicated."

"Talk to me, Cooper. We used to tell each other everything. I miss that." There's a quiver in Nattie's voice, and I hate knowing it's my fault.

"I love you, Nat. But around the time I realized girls had boobs, I stopped telling you everything." We both laugh, and my shoulders relax an inch. "I love her, Nat. That's pretty much all you need to know." Why the fuck I'm telling my sister, instead of Carys, is a whole other question, but I don't spend time figuring that out now. "We've both made mistakes, but she's it. We should have just told everyone last year, but Carys wasn't ready. And she was my priority."

Nattie gasps, and I prepare myself for the lecture that's about to come. "She's your Brady."

Well, hell . . . That's not at all what I was expecting and maybe not exactly how I'd put it. But she's not wrong. "Yeah, Nat. She is. But we've still got a ton of shit to work through. It might take us a while."

"Why, Coop? Why, after everything you've been

through, would you take that long? Don't get me wrong, I was so pissed when she stood up in Dad's kitchen and demanded to get on that jet, but it was really hurt masked as anger. I was so scared of losing you, then furious to find out you'd been keeping something so big from me. And there she was, an easy target to take it all out on in that moment. And you know what . . . ?"

Nattie waits, but I don't answer as I finally absorb what it must have felt like for them. Hearing it from the two most important women in my life brings it all home in a way nothing else has.

"She stood there, Coop. She stood there and took it, telling us all that she loved you and she was getting on that plane. She went right back at Murphy when he pissed her off in a way I didn't know Carys was capable of. She's always been so quiet when she wasn't on stage, which I guess, makes sense in a family as full of big personalities as ours is. But that day, she stood ten feet tall with tears falling in rivers down her face, and she might as well have told us all to fuck off because she was going to be by your side, one way or the other."

And I pushed her away. "That sounds like Carys to me."

"Funny. Because it didn't sound like Carys to *us*." Nat laughs. "I mean, I was pissed as hell that day. Truth be told, I was pissed until I saw her last week. But once I talked to her . . . and once I talked to Brady about it . . . it made sense. I wouldn't have let anyone keep me from him either. So, work it out, Cooper."

"It's not that easy, Nat." Might as well get it all out. "Listen, like I said, I haven't had a chance to talk to Declan yet, so this stays between us for now. I promise to call as soon as I can, but it might not be today."

My eyes catch on a teenager who walks slowly by,

along the sand. He's close to the gate but doesn't stop. I keep my eyes trained on him, and he keeps going down the beach.

"Earth to Cooper. I promise. Now keep going." I can't wait to see Nattie as a mom because she has the patience of a fruit fly.

"I was medically discharged from the Navy. There's an issue with my eyesight. Not major, but enough that I can't be a SEAL. And there's an issue with my last op. There's some pretty serious shit going on right now, so it's not as easy as you make it sound." Leaning back, I kick my legs out, stretching. "It's just not simple right now, Nat."

Nattie laughs again, but this time it's manic, bordering on hysterics. "Coop, you're in love with our stepsister." Another round of laughter bursts from her lips. "And you think it's going to be simple? Think again, little brother. You've got some ass-kissing to do before we all get over the fact you kept this from us."

"Hey," I cut in. "You may be three minutes older, but I'm bigger, and I'm not kissing anyone's ass."

"Sucks to be Carys, then. But seriously, how are you doing with the discharge? How are you feeling?" Damn, she can change moods on the drop of a dime.

"I'm still processing the discharge. It's going to take some time. But physically, I'm getting there." The teenager from earlier walks back into my line of sight, and I stand from my chair. "Listen, Nat. I've got to go."

"Try not to get into a fight with Murphy on Saturday, okay? Remember you both love her, and he's pissed as hell. Then maybe imagine if Brady had done what you did. And if all else fails, remember you're a trained killer, and he's our stepbrother and one of your best friends. I love you."

"Love you too, Nat. Talk soon." I step off the deck and

walk down the path to the gate. "Hey . . ." The kid in jeans and a white tank top turns my way, and he can't possibly be older than thirteen. "Need help finding something?"

"Yeah, actually." He adjusts his baseball cap and looks up at the house behind me. "Any chance you know a Cooper Sinclair?"

What the actual fuck?

"Yeah, I know him. Why are you looking for him?" I open the gate and take a step forward, towering over him, and cross my arms over my chest, flexing. Not sure why I feel the need to intimidate a kid, but something about this isn't right.

"Good." He pulls a crumbled-up envelope from his pocket and hands it to me. "Can you give this to him?" He takes a step back, then pivots to run, but he can't before I grab his shoulder.

"What the fuck is this?" I demand, my fury building without even looking at the contents. This is not good.

The kid tries to break my hold, but he's got no chance. "Some guy paid me fifty bucks to give that to you. He said I needed to put it in Cooper Sinclair's hand. Then he said you'd never admit it was you, just that you knew him. Dude, I don't want to get hurt. So, take it or don't. I don't give a shit if you're him. Just let me go." He jerks back, and I drop my hold, then watch him land on his ass in the sand.

"Get the fuck out of here and get a real job." The kid runs away, kicking sand up all around him, and I rip open the blank envelope. There's a single picture inside. It's of Carys, standing on her balcony last night with that damn shirt falling off her shoulder. The time stamp in the bottom corner is printed on it in blue, reading 2:17 a.m.

I flip it over and read the message printed in messy handwriting across the back.

Give me back what's mine before I take what's yours.
My stomach bottoms out as I look around.
I'm going to kill him.

CARYS

Emerson and I stare at Jessie, who's sitting on the floor, legs crossed, as she puts together a baby swing like she's done it a million times.

"You know you're strangely good at that, Jess." Emerson's milk has come in, so she's decided to try to nurse Elodie. She's currently lying on her side with her gigantic boob out while Elodie gets milk drunk. Her little eyes are heavy-lidded while her tiny fingers are wrapped around one of Em's. When Em looks up at me, she laughs. "What are you staring at, CC?"

"Seriously?" I tease her. "Your boobs are massive. They're bigger than Elodie's head."

"Don't be jealous, sister. They hurt like hell. That's why I'm nursing. I never thought I'd want to do this. It's strange. I sorta feel like a cow, but . . ." She looks down at her beautiful baby. "I kinda love it."

Emerson jerks her head toward Jessie when she sniffles. "What the hell, Jess? I'm the one who's supposed to be hormonal and crying, not you."

Jessie makes a noise that falls somewhere between a sob and a snort, then hides her face in her hands, laughing . . . I think.

"Oh my God. What was that?" I grab a pillow from the couch and toss it across the room at her.

Jessie catches it with ease, then holds it against her chest. "Sorry. I'm a mess." She's quiet for a moment, then smiles. "Ford and I didn't want to say anything until we were out of the first trimester. But I hit thirteen weeks a few days ago. So, I guess, *surprise*. I'm pregnant."

Emerson and I both squeal, and I jump off the couch to hug Jessie.

Elodie doesn't like the interruption and squawks like a baby bird, to make sure we all know she's unhappy about being disturbed, before Em lifts her to her shoulder to burp her.

"I'm so happy for you guys, Jess." We sway from side to side as we hug.

"Really?" she asks with a sadness to her voice.

Wow. What kind of friend am I that she even has to question that? "Yes. Really. This is fantastic news." I squeeze her. "Another baby to love."

A few months ago, it would have been harder news to handle.

Hell, it was harder news when my entire family decided being pregnant together was a fabulous thing. But I was never . . . not for one single moment, not happy for them.

Life has kicked my ass a little since then.

Priorities changed.

Just then, Rook comes out of the basement, where Ford, Cooper, and he have been hiding for the last hour.

Not sure if they're plotting world domination or figuring out how to kick Axel's ass, but something had Cooper worked up earlier.

Rook's eyes bug out of his head as he looks from a hugging Jess and me over to Emerson's giant boobs before averting his eyes and, I'm pretty sure, blushing. "I just wanted to grab a drink." He points toward the kitchen.

Em laughs. "Yeah, so did Elodie."

Jessie and I fall into a fit of giggles as Rook turns right

back around and heads back downstairs, slamming the door shut behind him.

"What are they doing down there anyway?" Em puts her boobs away and hands Elodie to me before she moves into the kitchen and pours herself a glass of water.

Jessie and I look at each other with trepidation.

They put Em on an antidepressant last night, and it should take a few days to kick in. In the meantime, she's really trying to get herself in a better place, and I worry that what I'm about to say is going to cause her to spiral. The Em we've had today has been very different from the one I've been around for the past week.

"There's some stuff going on that the guys are dealing with from the last op," I tell her, hoping she doesn't ask any questions but knowing Emerson well enough to know there's zero chance of that happening.

She lifts her glass to her lips, watching Jessie and me as she drinks the entire thing.

Her hand shakes as she sets the empty glass down on the marble counter, and then she places both palms flat on either side of it and levels us with an icy glare. "What kind of stuff?"

"Honey." Jessie moves to her side and rubs a hand over Emerson's back. "Why don't you sit down?"

Em shrugs her off, spinning away so fast her hair whips against Jessie's cheek. "I don't want to sit down. I don't want to be coddled. I want one of you to tell me what's going on. What do I not know?" Her face pales. "Oh God —" she breaks on a sob. "Does it have something to do with Linc?"

I consider putting Elodie in the swing, but I'm not sure if Jessie finished putting it together, so I shift her in my arms instead. "Em . . . I don't think either of us knows everything yet."

Jessie nods in agreement. "We don't. Ford refuses to tell me everything. But what we do know is that Axel has gone AWOL. And he's causing problems. I think that's what they're talking about."

"No." Em slaps her palm against the counter. "I'm not going to be kept in the dark in my own house. Especially not about something involving the death of my husband." She marches over to the basement door, a furious red suddenly coloring her previously pale cheeks.

But she doesn't have a chance to reach for it before it swings open and Ford steps through. He grabs Em's shoulders, steadying her, as Rook and Cooper move out around him. "You okay, Emerson?"

"No. I'm not okay. One of you needs to start talking now. I want to know what happened . . ." She swallows and takes a beat to gather herself. "What happened to Linc? And what's going on with Axel? This is my house, and you're not allowed to keep something from me in my own damn house. I don't care how big of an alpha male each one of you is. I will cut you down if I have to."

A look passes between the three guys before Ford clears his throat and motions for the couch. "Why don't you girls take a seat."

Emerson opens her mouth to protest, but Ford stops her. "Em, this isn't easy for any of us. If you want to hear this, you need to sit."

It's then that I see the fatigue on Ford's handsome face —the lines around his eyes and the tight set of his jaw as he tugs on Jessie's hair.

I move to the couch and sit down with Elodie, who's wide-awake, her violet eyes staring at me. "Come sit with me, Em."

Jessie moves next to Em and holds her hand as the two of them sit down next to me.

The guys follow them over, each choosing a different spot to stand. All are similarly posed with crossed arms and frustrated scowls.

My heart hurts, looking at them, as Ford speaks.

"There's only so much I can share and not get court-martialed for. You need to understand that." His eyes swing to Cooper's.

Coop scowls but speaks all the same, "*Right*. Well, the Navy's already kicked me to the curb, so I guess I'll fill in the blanks. But keep in mind, my fucked up brain doesn't remember any of this."

Pain ricochets through me at his words, and as if sensing my hurt, Elodie nuzzles her soft head into the crook of my neck.

Cooper watches me as he fills in what blanks he can, while silent tears fall all around. It's hard to believe any of us have any tears left to cry.

He fills in what he knows went down on the op and in Germany.

Then the way Axel approached me at the hospital.

But when he pauses and his eyes flare, I know there something else, even if he won't say it.

Instead, Rook steps forward, adding, "We have something Axel wants back. But we can't give it to him. We have connections trying to locate him, so he can pay for his crimes. But it could take a few days."

The room sits silent until Emerson stands and reaches down to take Elodie from me. She doesn't look at Cooper or Ford. Instead, she walks right up to Rook, fury filling her face. "Promise me he's going to pay."

"I promise," Rook answers without hesitation.

She nods her head in acceptance. "He loved you guys. You know that, right? He said you were the only family he had. That you were his brothers. Don't let him down."

A dark expression stretches across Cooper's face as he takes that hit and rolls with it.

I love my friend, but she didn't need to say that. These guys have already taken this on themselves more than I think we'll ever know. I know Coop blames himself. He might not have said it, but it's obvious.

I wish I could take away all his pain.

Take away the hurt of the last few months and rewind the clock.

But that's not an option.

I guess I need to love him through it, the way he wanted to do for me, and hope he's less of a stubborn fool than I was.

COOPER

Once Ford and Jessie leave, Rook walks over to the fridge. "What are we doing for dinner?"

Emerson yawns from the couch, while she feeds Elodie under a light blanket Carys laid over them for privacy before going upstairs. "I'm actually starving. Can we order out? I don't want any of that funeral food. I could go for pizza."

"Thank fuck. I thought you were going to say sushi or some shit like that." Rook pulls out his phone and calls it in. "I'm gonna go grab my bag from the truck."

Emerson's nearly purple eyes sharpen, focused on me. "Why is Rook getting a bag? What's in it?"

"He's going to crash here for a few days. That way, one of us can always be with you girls." Judging by the venomous expression on her face, I'm glad I'm not within reach right now.

"Do you think one of you assholes could check with me before you make decisions for me?" She asks the question quietly to not upset the baby, but she's definitely pissed. "I know I've been a mess, but I'm an adult. I'm a fucking mother. Do not handle me, Sinclair, or you won't be happy with the result." She pulls Elodie out from under the blanket and throws it over her shoulder as she burps the baby. "And I'm not going to smother my baby under a blanket just because two grown men can't handle boobs."

Rook walks back in and rolls his neck before a wicked

129

grin stretches across his face. "Those aren't boobs. Those are watermelons on steroids, woman."

I expect her to catapult herself over the couch and attack, but Elodie exhales a burp that puts the rest of us to shame, and we all burst out laughing.

Emerson looks at her chest, like it's the first time she's seen it, and pulls some little circular pad thing from her bra, then throws it at Rook, smacking him in the face. "Asshole. They're the best goddamn watermelons you'll never get to taste."

He holds up the soaked circle. "What is this?"

Carys walks back downstairs with her sketch pad in hand. She grabs the circle thing from Rook and winces. "Why do you have Emerson's nursing pad?"

"Her what?" Rook's expression transforms from confusion to mortification pretty damn quick.

Carys bites her bottom lip, trying to mask her laughter, then pats Rook's chest with her free hand. "When a woman nurses a baby, her other boob leaks. This sucker . . ." She holds it up in front of Rook's face. "Is drenched with breast milk."

"Fucking gross," he gags.

"It's nature, Rook. Get over it." She slaps the pad back into his hand, then moves next to the couch. "I've got to get some sketching done." She trails a finger along Elodie's black hair. "Do you need anything, Em?"

"No, thanks. I'm going to try to put her down for a bit and crash until the pizza gets here." Emerson rises from the couch and adjusts the baby. "On second thought, I'm going to sleep until she wakes up. I can always heat the pizza up. Just don't let the guys eat it all."

Carys leans in and kisses the top of Elodie's head, then heads for the back door.

"Hey, where are you going?" Not my smoothest line.

Her brows shoot up, and she cocks her hip. "I was going outside to sketch. Is that a problem?"

I haven't told her about the picture I got this morning.

Guess there's no time like the present.

"We need to talk, Carys." I reach for her, but she takes a step away, her sharp eyes questioning me.

"That doesn't sound good, Coop." She looks around as Rook escapes upstairs.

When I step closer, she stays put and allows me to wrap my fingers around her delicate arms. "I'm concerned Axel is going to use you to get to me. He's already approached you at the hospital, and he—"

My girl doesn't cower when she cuts me off. Her glittering green eyes dance between mine. "Why?"

"What?" I have no idea what she's getting at.

"Why would he use me? I'm nothing, remember?" She dares me to correct her, and I take the damn bait.

My hands slide up her arms and neck, then into her hair. "You could never be nothing, Carys, and you know it."

One side of her mouth tips up into a cautious smile. "I had my hopes."

"He threatened you this morning." I hold her head possessively and wait for her to freak out. But it doesn't come.

"He threatened me at the hospital too, didn't he? I might not have known it then, but I figured it out after you told me what was going on. I'm safe here with you. You won't let anything happen to me." She turns her head and kisses my hand. "I'll go sketch in my room."

"So you're not mad then?" I wasn't expecting her to take this so well, but like always, she continually surprises me.

"Mad? *No.* Do I have the heebie jeebies about this whole thing? *Yes*, I do. But it'll be over soon." Glad she's so sure because I'm not there yet.

"Stay inside, okay?" I think of the picture, and my adrenaline pumps with fury. "Make sure your balcony door is locked."

"You know how I love bossy Cooper." Her teeth dig into her bottom lip, and the little brat practically skips up the stairs.

The rest of the night is uneventful.

Carys has decided to sleep in Emerson's room to help her with Elodie.

So I chose to sleep on the couch tonight. She offered me her bed, but it didn't feel right, and I'm not sure why. Hours later, as I lie here, staring at the ceiling, I realize it's because I want to be lying in bed with her.

It will always be her.

Was I holding back to protect Carys? Or myself?

The thoughts consume me as I try to sleep.

I've only just closed my eyes sometime after midnight, when movement on the stairs wakes me up, and my eyes strain to see who it is. I sit up as my eyes adjust and realize it's the woman occupying my thoughts. "Carys?"

She's walking toward me in my old high-school football shirt, with Elodie curled into a tiny ball against her chest, and she's singing softly to the baby.

She stops in front of me, and I reach a hand out. Unable to stop myself from touching her, I run it up the back of her bare thigh. "Is everything okay?"

"Shh . . . Everything's fine," she whispers. "Em just fed her, and Elodie was fussing, so I thought I'd give her a break and take the baby." The moonlight filters in through the windows, bathing her in a silver glow. Her messy hair tumbles around her shoulders, and her green eyes sparkle. She looks angelic as she stands in front of me, swaying with an unhappy baby.

"Does she have one of those binky things the twins had when they were little? The things they suck on?" I try to keep my eyes on hers, but the shirt barely comes to the tops of her thighs, and there's no way I can't notice when those bare legs are right in front of my face.

"Oh, she does. Let me go find it . . . Here." She lays Elodie against my bare chest, then steps back and sighs a sweet sigh. "I think my ovaries just exploded."

"Is that bad?" *Fuck.* What if she gets sick now?

Carys giggles, and damn, what that sound does to me. "No, Cooper. It's not bad." Her eyes soften, and she licks her lips. "I'm going to see if the hospital sent home a binky."

Her ass cheeks peek out with each stair she climbs, and my mouth waters.

Elodie farts, then makes a noise that sounds like she's laughing at herself.

Can babies laugh?

I look down at her, and her violet eyes are staring back at me, wide open. "So that's what you think of me, huh, kid?" I stand from the couch and sway side to side the way Emerson and Carys do when they're holding her. Hoping it keeps her happy. "Your dad used to laugh when he farted too. He liked to make us all laugh, and he was good at it. He was good at a lot of things. He loved you. Your mom sent him pictures of you in her belly every week. Just so he wouldn't miss a thing. He wanted to give you all the things he never had. Talked about it all the time."

He should be here now, holding her. Not me. "I promise I'll tell you all about him, okay?" I kiss her head when she fidgets against me, and my heart melts as she stills. Those eyes are Emerson's, but man, she looks so much like Linc.

By the time Carys comes downstairs with a green binky in her hand, Elodie has fallen asleep, and I've fallen completely in love with this tiny human.

"You're a natural, Coop." She stands in front of me and covers Elodie in a tiny pink-and-white blanket. "Want me to take her from you?"

"Nah." I sit down in the corner of the couch and kick my legs up on the ottoman. "I've got her. Let her sleep."

"You look good holding her." She sits down next to me, and our legs touch, sending an extra buzz of awareness through my skin. "How's your incision feel?"

"Better every day." *Mostly*. "The headaches are still there, but they said that could take a few more weeks."

Carys moves her hand behind my head and starts massaging the base of my skull, and I moan. "Tell me about being home before . . ." I leave off the rest.

We both know I mean before the op.

Before the call.

Before Linc died.

"Chloe and I are working on a new line, using the most gorgeous French lace I've ever seen. It's teal and black. It reminds me of the feather I found on the beach that night last year." Her fingers stop for a second. "Do you remember?"

"Like I could ever forget." I turn my head to her. "That feather's been on every mission with me since you gave it to me."

"Coop . . ." Her hand drops away, and she stands, pulling away emotionally and physically. "I'm going to take Elodie back upstairs." She scoops the baby out of my arms and doesn't look back.

I stand and follow her to the stairs. "Who's running now, Carys?"

Carys turns slowly toward me. "I'm right here, fighting for us. But you need to figure out if you love me or hate me, Coop. Because this . . ." She motions between the two of us. "This back-and-forth, where I think I'm getting somewhere with you and then you push me away . . . That hurts. And I'm too tired tonight for hurt. Honestly, I don't know how much more of it I can take without breaking."

She leans in on shaky legs and kisses my cheek. "I know what I want, and I'll fight for it, but don't keep giving me hope and then tearing it away."

"I wasn't trying to do that . . ."

Carys places a hand on my chest. "I know. But that's exactly what you're doing. I'm here. I'm not going anywhere. And I love you. Now, it's time for *you* to figure out how you feel." She drops her hand and turns around, taking Elodie back upstairs.

I watch her as she slips back into Emerson's room and closes the door behind her.

I already know how I feel. It's time to stop holding back.

I'm done watching this woman walk away.

CARYS

I may still be heartbroken over the fact I'll never carry my own baby, but thirty-six hours of helping Emerson with Elodie has me wanting to sleep for a week.

So heartbroken, yes.

In a rush for a baby, no.

I just finished showering for the second time today because Elodie spit up in my hair. The smell is still stuck in my nostrils. But I somehow managed to pull myself together enough for dinner with Aiden. *Begrudgingly.* I still don't know if this is a good idea.

When the doorbell rings a few minutes later, I guess it's too late to cancel.

I hurry down the stairs and come face-to-face with my brother, who's holding a crying Elodie, and for a moment, I remember he's only a few months away from becoming a father himself.

"She's perfect, Emerson." Aiden gives the baby back to Em, then smiles at me. It's not his normal over-the-top smile, but it's a start. "Hey, Care Bear."

"Hey." I stretch up on my toes and kiss his cheek.

Aiden picks up the two take-out bags from the Italian place down the street and holds them up for me. "Hope you're in the mood for pasta. I wasn't sure what everyone wanted, so I got a little bit of everything."

"Thanks." I take one from him and start emptying it on

the kitchen island. "Em, could you let Cooper know Aiden's here, please?"

"Guess that answers my first question." Aiden grinds his teeth, and I sigh.

"And what question is that?" I ask, already annoyed and readying for the confrontation I know is coming, while I continue emptying both take-out bags.

Aiden opens the containers, then starts opening drawers and slamming them shut as he looks for silverware. Once he finds what he's looking for, he lifts his head. "Whether or not you and Cooper are together."

"If you have a question, ask it." I ignore the rest of his mini-tantrum as I grab a stack of plates and put them next to the food. "Do you want something to drink?"

"Water's fine." He helps himself to a bottle from the fridge, then glares as Rook and Cooper enter the room.

Em stands next to me, and I tickle Elodie's chubby little legs. "Want me to take her so you can eat something?" I ask, hoping to avoid the conversation from hell I'm about to have.

"Nope." She hip-checks me. "Why don't you three take your plates outside for privacy. Rook and I can stay in here."

Rook offers Aiden his hand. "Rook."

"Aiden. Nice to meet you." They shake, and Aiden fills his plate, then hands it to me. "Mom said you've lost too much weight and need to eat."

I refuse to take it from him. "Mom's insane, and I don't ever eat that much. I can make my own plate, thanks." I pick up a plate and hand it to Cooper before getting one for myself. Thick waves of tension radiate off all of us. "Does anyone want wine?"

Aiden and Cooper both answer no.

"More for me." I pour myself a glass of red and take it

and my plate out on to the porch, half expecting Cooper to say it's not safe. But he doesn't. He just follows me out, his eyes alert and assessing.

The three of us sit down around the table without anyone saying a word.

Oh, what the hell . . .

"So how was your flight?" Great. I've been reduced to small talk with my brother.

Aiden puts his fork down, his gaze locked on me. "How long have you two been together?"

"Guess we're getting right to it then?" I take a sip of my wine, planning to answer, but Cooper beats me to it.

"A year and a half." Coop hasn't touched his plate. He sits, staring at Aiden. Alpha male energy out in full force. It's like watching two male gorillas circle each other at the zoo.

This is so not going to go well.

Aiden's posture straightens. "Eighteen months and you never thought to tell me?" His question is directed at Cooper . . . until his eyes swing to me. "Either of you?"

"That was my fault," I admit.

"It was not," Cooper deflects the attention from me. "We're adults, Murph. We made the decision we thought was right for us. We didn't want to involve any of you until we were ready. It might not have been the right thing for you, but it was the right thing for us."

Aiden looks up to the sky and blows out a breath, then nails us with his anger. "You're full of shit. You and I both know it."

"Aiden . . ." I stop him, but he ignores me and keeps his focus on Cooper.

"You're a hypocrite. All these years of busting Brady's balls for being with Nattie, and we all laughed about it. But at least he did that to your face. He didn't hide it. He didn't disrespect you or Nattie. You're worse than a hypocrite because Brady respected you enough to ask for permission to date your sister. He kept it all out in the open. You didn't even respect Carys enough to do that."

I throw my napkin on the table and slap my palm against it. "What is wrong with you? I'm a grown woman. No man needs to ask my brother for permission to date me, Aiden James. And he respected me so much that he respected *my wishes* and didn't tell you. That was my choice. Not his."

Aiden throws his hands into the air. "What the actual fuck, Carys?"

"Watch it," Cooper growls.

Aiden's eyes soften for a minute. "I don't care how old you are, Carys. You will always be my little sister. It's my job to protect you. And he . . ." Then he turns his anger back on Cooper. "You broke the fucking code. She's younger than you, and she's your goddamn sister." His voice grows louder with each angry word. "That's some fucked up shit."

I reach over and shove Aiden away as I rise from the table. "I'm two years younger than you, asshole. Sabrina is only fifteen fucking months older than me, and you married her and knocked her up already. What's the difference?" I yell back at him just as loud.

"Sabrina's not my sister." His smug face fuels my anger.

I lower my voice until it's eerily calm. "He's my *stepbrother*, and he was already out of the house before Mom and Coach got married. Don't make this into something it's not."

Aiden stands, towering over me. "Don't argue semantics, Carys. What he did was wrong."

Coop's chair screeches as he stands and shoves it back. "Who the fuck are you to decide what's right and wrong,

Murph? You banged everything with a heartbeat back in school. You didn't even know half their names. I never disrespected a woman like that." Cooper crosses his thick arms over his chest and moves around me so that he stands toe-to-toe with Aiden. "Hell, you thought you got a girl pregnant, and you didn't even remember her name when she told you about it. Don't think any of us forgot about that."

Well, shit. That's news to me.

"You found Sabrina, and everything changed. Because she was your girl, and you fucking knew it." Cooper's body is coiled tight like a snake ready to attack.

"You're revising history, *brother*." The word is spit out of Aiden's mouth in disgust. "You were no saint."

"You fucked your way through senior year," Cooper yells.

Murphy holds his ground. "You fucked my sister."

I gasp, and the backyard goes jarringly silent until Cooper takes one impossible step closer to Aiden. "Don't ever say anything like that about her again, or I will fucking kill you." His words are calm and controlled. Spoken slowly, making them even scarier. "I love you, brother, but I love *her* more. Don't let there be a next time, or I will rip your throat out with my bare hands. Do you understand?"

I close my eyes for a minute and let his words wash over me, mending all the frayed edges of my soul. When I open them, Aiden has a goofy smile on his face, but Cooper is definitely still furious.

"You love my sister?" Aiden asks, his entire demeanor changed.

Without skipping a beat, Cooper answers, "More than anyone ever will."

I take a stuttered breath for what feels like the first time in months as I fight to hold back the tears threatening to break free. Relief washing over me.

"Wait . . . wait . . . wait . . ." Aiden's smile grows. "You realize, if you get married, you're marrying *your* sister?" Oh. My. God. He's giving me whiplash.

Cooper rolls his eyes and shoves Aiden's chest, like they didn't just almost come to blows. "When I marry her, I'll be marrying the woman I love. My sister . . ." He looks at me, and the undeniable warmth in his eyes leaves me breathless. "My *only* sister is already married, asshole."

"So, if you have kids—"

I smack my brother. "Enough."

He turns his sarcastic glare my way. "The fuck it is. If he loves you, I can't be mad at him. But *you* assholes kept this from all of us for a long time. You were both in my wedding, and we had no idea."

I clench my thighs, remembering the things Cooper did to me the night of Aiden and Sabrina's rehearsal dinner and smother the moan that threatens to erupt. When I look up, Coop's smirking at me. No doubt in my mind, he knows exactly what I'm thinking.

My clueless brother pulls me in for a hug, having no idea the filthy fantasy I lived out that night. He groans as he squeezes my shoulder, "You had to work to keep it from us, and I'm not gonna lie and say that didn't hurt. We're never letting you live this down. It's already been decided." He slings his arm around Cooper's shoulders and leaves his other around me. "The others aren't even pissed. Not really. But we're gonna give you hell for the rest of your lives over this shit."

Cooper shrugs out of Aiden's hold. "Whatever you say, Murph."

"Seriously . . . you're in love with your sister. Come on," Aiden jokes.

Cooper's eyes turn hungry as he approaches me. "No, asshole. I'm in love with *your* sister."

He steps between my brother and me, then slides his hand around my neck and squeezes before he kisses me. His lips brush over mine, and butterflies take flight in my stomach as I wrap myself around him and get lost in the moment.

"Okay, okay. Enough. I get the picture." We both ignore Aiden, savoring this kiss.

When I pull back from Cooper, breathless and dying to lock us in a room for the night, Aiden's already sitting back down, eating his dinner. He looks up at us with a fork full of chicken parmigiana halfway to his mouth. "Are you done yet?"

"Oh, big brother. Every single time you torture us about being stepsiblings, I'm going to torture you in a totally different way. You already caught Mom and Coach banging in the kitchen. I'll make that look like a Disney movie." I sit down next to Aiden and lay my napkin back down in my lap.

His face pales. "You wouldn't."

"Oh, but I would." Two can play at this game.

COOPER

MURPHY GOT OVER EVERYTHING FASTER THAN I EXPECTED.

He's always been the biggest hothead among us.

And he wasn't wrong.

If Brady had tried hiding his relationship with Nattie, I'd have been beyond pissed.

But I'd do it all again if it meant I got to keep Carys at the end of it all.

Because I'm not letting go this time. Not ever again. This woman is mine. She's always been, and I want every fucking person around us to know it too.

So hours later, when Carys shuts the front door behind Murphy, I claim her.

I spin her around and crowd her body against the door —one palm flat on the wood next to her face, the other on her hip, with my knees bent, bringing myself eye level with my beautiful girl. Fighting for the control that snapped hours ago and has been teetering on the brink since.

She gasps and brings her soft hands up, running her fingers through my hair. The tenderness in her eyes overwhelms me. "You love me?"

"You are the air I breathe, Carys Murphy. Did you ever really doubt it? I needed to get my head on straight." I run my nose along her neck, inhaling her. "You've got to realize we're still in the middle of a storm, baby, but I never stopped loving you. You—loving you, protecting you above everything else in this life—that will always be my top priority." I lean in and take her lips in a punishing kiss, my tongue stroking hers.

Our bodies pressed together. Leaving no room between us.

Her soft curves melt against me, and my cock strains to get closer.

It's frenzied and messy. Urgent and needy.

Carys whimpers in my arms. "God, Cooper." She licks into my mouth, pushing for more and wraps her arms around my neck, rubbing against me.

Until I'm not sure where she stops and I start.

My hands slide down her body and under her dress, gripping her ass and squeezing.

Needing to feel her skin against me.

I lift her as she wraps herself around me like a koala bear, and the heat of her pussy has my cock pulsing in response. "I missed you, baby," I groan against her skin.

She nips at my ear as I walk us up the stairs. "Every day, Cooper." She bites my earlobe and tugs it between her teeth, then runs her tongue along the edge. "I missed you when you were gone . . ."

I step into her room and kick the door shut behind us, then turn her back against it for leverage.

Carys rips my shirt over my head and kisses me again, her tongue sweeping into my mouth in hot, frantic strokes. "I missed you even more when you were next to me and I couldn't touch you. I never want to feel that kind of pain again." She pulls her dress over her head, then unbuckles my belt and unzips my jeans. "Touch me," she begs. "Please God, touch me before I die."

We shove my jeans down just enough, and I rip her panties from her body and take her mouth again as I drag my cock through her soaked pussy. My head spins as all the blood in my body rushes to my dick with an urgent need.

I drag my tongue down her delicate neck, then bite down on the crease by her shoulder as I drive into her, burying myself. Drowning in her.

Carys winces as her tight little pussy adjusts to my cock after having gone months without each other. We both still. Reveling in the connection between us.

Silent.

Motionless.

She feels like fucking heaven and tastes like sin.

I have to take a minute before I move, or this'll be over before it starts.

Electricity sparks and soars between us, as lightning pulls at my spine.

Need and want outweigh my hesitation as I tug her bottom lip between my teeth. "Are you okay, baby?" I'm holding onto my composure by a worn, fraying thread.

"Fuck me, Cooper," she demands as her nails score my back and her heels dig into my ass. She grinds down on my cock, unleashing a fire that incinerates my composure, and singes my skin.

I set a punishing rhythm, fucking away the hurt and anger between us.

My muscles contract with every snap of my hips. Mind-numbing pain mixes with soul-burning pleasure as we fuck our way into oblivion. "You feel that, baby? You feel us?"

She nods her head. "Don't stop, Coop," she moans. "I'm close." Her pussy clenches around me.

I wrap my arms around her tiny waist and move her so only her shoulder blades touch the door. Changing the angle. Going deeper.

Carys's eyes flutter shut, as her arms curl around my shoulders, and she moans as she comes.

Pulling her body against mine, I take two quick steps across the room and toss her on the bed. "Up on all fours, baby."

She quickly scurries across the bed, putting her ass in the air. Then she flips her hair to look up at me over her shoulder.

My mouth goes dry at the sight in front of me. This beautiful woman. Open and vulnerable.

I step out of my jeans and drag my hand across the globes of her ass, then spank her with a quick snap of my wrist.

Carys drops her forehead to the mattress and fists the sheets as she cries out, then backs up, looking for more. "Please, Cooper," she begs, and I kiss the red handprint standing out in stark contrast to her pale skin.

"Please what, baby?" I fist my cock and place a knee on the bed, then smack the other side. "You gonna get scared and run again, Carys?" I dip my face down, inhaling her intoxicating scent, and growl against her pussy as her juices coat my face.

"Ohmygod . . ." she cries out. "Now, Coop. Please, God. Now."

I pull back and drag a thumb through the evidence of her orgasm, then up around the tight ring of her ass, running it around the puckered skin before pushing it in.

Carys thrashes against the bed, incoherent, as I plunge my cock into her pussy while my thumb fucks her ass.

My dick weeps from the hot, wet, vise-like grip she's got on me. I set a hungry rhythm as I wrap her silky hair around my fist and pound into her, tugging her up so she arches her back.

She pushes back to meet me with every hard thrust.

Her body already shaking.

Breathing in rapid, heavy breaths as she keens.

"Never again, Carys," I tell her as I lean over her and kiss my way up her spine until my mouth is next to hers. "It's us, baby. It's always gonna be us." I take her mouth in a vicious kiss.

Her body quivers for me as she whimpers, and my heart pounds a drumbeat against my chest. "I'm never letting you go again, Coop." Her voice is thready. On edge. She's there.

I shift behind her. Dragging my cock inside her. Fucking her. Loving her. "You take my cock like such a good girl, baby."

Carys's orgasm rolls through her shaking body, milking me, while white-hot blistering pleasure pulls at my spine, and my orgasm rushes through me.

We fall to the bed in a tangle of arms and legs, breathing heavy, and I pull her back against my chest.

Once we can both breathe again, my lips caress the shell of her ear. "Never again, baby. It's us against the world."

"You and me, Coop. No running. From either of us." She twists her head and kisses me, soft and slow. Quieting the demons and soothing my soul.

CARYS

As my heart finally slows down, Elodie's cry registers in my brain. Flaming heat climbs up my face as I hide it against Cooper's chest and snicker. "I guess I wasn't exactly quiet."

He kisses the top of my head like it's the most natural thing in the world, and I melt into him. "No, babe. You weren't quiet."

I pop my head up and smile at the cocky grin plastered on his face, dragging the tip of my finger over his lips. "Thank you for not giving up on me, Cooper. I was a fool, and I was so scared it was too late to fix it."

One rough hand dances down my spine, while the other is tucked behind his head, stretching the tape over his healing wound tight against his skin.

Jesus. We didn't even think about his injury.

"Just promise me you'll talk to me next time, Carys. I need to know you trust me enough to believe I can handle anything thrown our way." He gently presses his palm against my back, pulling me closer. "The good and the bad, baby."

I rest my arms over his chest and press my lips to his. "There's going to be a lot of bad days, Coop. It's a lot to ask of you." My voice trembles with the honesty in my words. "I'm doing okay managing my lupus now, but I don't know what next week or next year looks like."

"Then we'll handle it together. I will always be right

next to you. And don't, for one minute, think you're the only one with baggage. You might have been the one a little unsure of your life *last* year, but I have to come up with a whole new game plan for my life *this* year." His fingers dance up my spine, sending shivers down my skin.

"I've got no fucking clue what I'm doing or where I'll end up. And with this shit with Axel still hanging over our heads, I haven't even had time to think about it." His tired eyes close, and stress lines pull tight around them.

I swing a leg over his hips, being careful of the bandage further up his ribs, and rub myself over his impressive cock. "If you're this stressed-out right now, I must have done something very wrong," I tease.

Coop's hands grasp my waist, and he adjusts me so the head of his dick nudges against my entrance. "Ready for round two, Miss Murphy?" His voice is raspy with desire, and those baby-blue eyes I love are drowning with need.

I steady my hands on his chest as I slide down his shaft, amazed at how hard he is for me already. "I'm always ready for you, Cooper," I whisper as I feel him filling me. "I was made for you."

"You're fucking right you are." He jackknifes up and wraps his arms around my back, bringing us chest-to-chest as I rock against him. Clinging to each other. "You're the other half of my soul, baby. The air I breathe."

With a hand holding the back of my neck in a tight grip, he brings my lips to his. Soft but powerful and achingly intoxicating.

When we breathe each other in, I'm flooded with tantalizing sensations, heightened by every hungry stroke of his tongue.

Hyperaware of every long drag of my body against his.

Luxuriating in each roll of my hips and drag of his tongue.

We take our time, teasing and tasting.

Taking my breath away while he breathes life back into me.

Cooper's hand skims up my body and around the back of my neck, while his thumb presses down on my pulse as it thrums wildly against my skin.

I move my body slowly, dragging out each movement as he slides his hand around the front of my throat. The tips of his fingers tightening slightly. Pressing in just enough . . .

Restricting my breathing.

Controlling my movement.

Heightening every sensation.

"Tighter," I whisper, my eyes locked on his.

His possessive look is holding me captive as he tightens his grip the slightest bit, and my pussy pulses in response around his cock.

The intensity of this moment becomes more charged than anything I've ever felt before.

We move agonizingly slowly. Our bodies dragging against each other. Every shallow breath I take lights me on fire, bringing me closer to orgasm as a boom of thunder outside my window shakes the room, just before a crack of lightning spotlights the night's sky.

Coop steals my soul when he takes my lips, and my vision closes in.

My body tightens around him as he growls against my mouth.

Rain dances against the glass doors. "I love you," I whisper breathlessly as a moan slips past my lips. Cooper lets go of my throat, and I shatter around him as fireworks burst behind my eyes.

Cooper gathers my face in his hands and holds my half-lidded gaze with his as he surges up once more and then comes with my name on his lips like a silent prayer.

I don't know how I ever thought I could live without this man.

When I wake up the next morning, I'm not surprised to find the other side of the bed empty. Judging by the sun trying to fight its way through the clouds, it's got to be mid-morning, and after the incredible night we had, I don't feel remotely guilty for sleeping away half the day.

I stand and stretch, enjoying the way my body aches, reminding me of all the ways I used it last night. I should really go for a run since I haven't done that in the last week but decide instead to take a long, hot shower, wishing Coop was up here to join me.

Twenty minutes later, I've got a little extra pep in my step when I open my door and Elodie's fussing carries down the hall. Emerson's door is open when I step into her room, and I find Elodie tucked inside the bassinet, while her momma stares inside her closet. "Hey, you okay, Em?"

Em turns toward me in a daze. "Yeah . . . I was just thinking I'm not supposed to be here." She looks around her room, like it's the first time she's seeing it. "We rented a place. We lived somewhere else, but when Linc—" She covers her mouth and closes her eyes. "When it happened, I came home with Jack and Theo and never left. Jack moved some of my stuff here. But most of it's still at my place."

Elodie lets out a shriek, and I pick her up. "Okay, sweetheart. What can Auntie Carys do for you?" I nuzzle my nose against her face as I hold her to my chest and sit on the bed to change her diaper.

"I have a nursery set up at home." Em watches the two of us with sad eyes. "Pale pinks and greens, and this gorgeous chiffon bunting hanging from the ceiling over a white sleigh crib. Dad's girlfriend hooked me up with an interior designer friend of hers, and she took care of it all. I never told Linc about it because he'd have been upset that I was spending money like that. He wanted to provide everything for us."

She sits down next to me and hands me a wipe. "I'm going to have to go home soon, aren't I?"

"No. There's no timetable for what feels right. You'll know when you're ready to go back there. And I'll be here to help you every step of the way." I finish changing Elodie's diaper, then snap the buttons on her onesie and pick her back up.

"You can't put your life on hold indefinitely, Carys. As much as I know you'd do it in a heartbeat, it's not fair to you." She trails a finger down Elodie's back.

I stand and sway back and forth with the baby, trying to keep her content while her momma has a few minutes to melt down. "It's not indefinitely. It's just the first few weeks when you have to have help, Em. Now, why don't you get a shower while Elodie and I go downstairs and hunt for the boys."

"Is that your way of saying I smell?" She stands and cocks a hip, then checks for herself and smells her armpit. "Okay. Yes, I need a shower. But first, I need to know how last night went?"

My cheeks flush, thinking about the way Coop and I reached for each other all night.

"Oh, come on," Emerson groans. "I know how *that* part of your night went. Everyone within a five-mile radius has no doubt about just how well it went. Girl, I don't remember you being that loud before."

I have to stop myself from commenting back about how loud she and Linc used to be. "Sorry about that." I blush harder.

"No, you're not. And I don't blame you one bit. Honestly, you could cut the freaking sexual tension around here with a chainsaw yesterday, it was so damn thick. But I was talking about your brother." She walks into her bathroom, leaving the door open. "How was Aiden last night?"

The water turns on, and Elodie and I walk to the door of the bathroom. "It went well. Why don't you take a shower, then try to get some sleep. I'll bring her back up when she needs to eat again. Does two hours-ish sound about right?"

Em peeks out and kisses her daughter's head. "You're a lifesaver, Carys. But I'm not letting you save my life at the cost of your own. Remember that." She steps back into the bathroom, closing the door behind her.

Elodie's big violet eyes look up at me, and I swear she smiles. "Come on, baby girl. Auntie Carys needs to find Uncle Coop." A smile spreads across my face when I realize I can't remember the last time I was this happy.

COOPER

"HEY, MAN. DID YOU HEAR TRICK IS BEING SENT STATESIDE for rehab next week?" I stare at Rook, who's cutting his omelet into perfectly portioned squares. I've never met anyone as regimented as he is, and that's saying something since I've been in the Navy for four years.

His forks stops halfway to his mouth, and his forehead wrinkles. "No. The fucker didn't tell me. Is he being discharged?"

I shrug. "Don't know. He texted, and trust me, that's not the kind of thing you want to talk about in a text."

"Sorry, man. Have you given any thought to what you want to do?" He shifts uncomfortably because this whole conversation sucks. Well, at least it does for me.

"Not really. This was it." I push my empty plate aside and pick up my coffee. "This was the plan. I didn't have a backup. I figured I had another fifteen years before I had to figure out what came after the teams."

Rook watches my movement with a question on the tip of his tongue.

You don't serve together as closely as we have and not learn each other's ticks. At least, that's what I'd have said before our last op. "Ask your question, brother. I can tell you have one."

"Have you talked to anyone yet?" I open my mouth to answer him, but he cuts me off, annoyed. "I don't mean one of us, shithead. I mean a shrink."

"Have you?" I counter. "I'm not the only one who lost something on that mission. And I'm aware enough to know that not only did I lose my job and a piece of my identity, but I also lost two friends. Not just one."

"Point taken." He takes a card out of his pocket and slides it across the table to me. "She comes highly recommended. I've spoken to a few guys who actually didn't hate talking to her. You gotta talk to someone, Coop, or you're gonna explode, man."

I stare at the card for a long beat before picking it up and flipping it over. "I'll think about it."

"Good." He points his fork at me. "You know . . ." His head snaps up at the sound of Elodie crying upstairs, then mumbles something about babies.

"Do I know what?" I prod, curious about where his head is.

He watches me as he finishes his eggs, then washes it down with an entire bottle of OJ. "Phoenix is looking to expand."

It's my turn to study him, and something twists in my stomach.

I hadn't thought about going into the private sector. I'm not sure I want to.

"I was going to finish our deployment, then get out. But since we've been sent home and currently have no team, I'm putting my retirement papers in when we clean up the Axel shitstorm. You could come with me."

We both turn as Carys skips down the stairs, singing a soft song to Elodie. She crosses the room and stops next to me, then drops a kiss on my lips. "Good morning."

Rook coughs to hide his laugh, and I expect Carys to be embarrassed, but my girl surprises me when she kicks his foot. "Whatever. Don't be jealous, soldier boy. In fact . . ."

She carefully transfers Elodie to Rook's arms and sashays into the kitchen.

One of my t-shirts is tucked into black leggings, cupping her ass perfectly, and my eyes stay glued to her as Rook grumbles about holding Elodie.

Carys makes herself a cup of tea, then joins us at the table. "Any chance Elodie and I can read a book outside for a little while? I could use some fresh air."

I glance over at Rook, who shakes his head.

"Probably not the best move, Carys." I grip her hips and pull her down on my lap.

"Fine," she huffs. "What are you guys doing today?"

I run my nose along her neck, and Rook groans, so I take Carys's lips in a quick kiss and give Rook the finger. "We've got data to work through."

"What does that mean?" She scrunches her nose, like an afternoon on a computer sounds awful to her.

"It means you need to get off your man's lap and grab this baby." He shifts Elodie carefully in his arms and lets her wrap her tiny fingers around his pinky. "I don't do babies, no matter how much you try to force it. I already pulled the short straw and agreed to drive Emerson to the pediatrician tomorrow. And seriously, didn't this kid just get out of the hospital? Why does she already have to see a doctor and be around all those germs?"

"Fine." She stands and lifts Elodie, then stage whispers, "I think you're wearing him down, sweetheart."

Elodie rests against Carys's chest, quiet and sleepy. It paints a pretty picture. Not that I'm ready for kids. I'll leave that to my siblings for a while. "What are your plans today, Carys?"

"I told Em to take a nap. Once she wakes up, I need to get a little sketching in. I promised Chloe I'd work on a few things this week, and the week's already over." She grabs a banana from the table and hands it to me. "Can you peel that for me, please?"

I guess it's kinda hard to do one-handed. I hand her back the peeled banana, and instead of taking it from me, she bites it right out of my hand. "How's that been going? Le Désir?"

She takes another bite and smiles. "It was so much easier when we were both in Kroydon Hills." Then she bites her lip, realizing what she just said. "Don't get me wrong. I love being here, and I'm so happy to help. But we had a process in place the past few months, and it worked really well."

Rook grabs our plates and takes them into the kitchen, leaving us alone.

"You want to move back to Kroydon Hills?" I watch her face, wanting to know the truth. Hoping she won't just say what she thinks I want to hear.

She sways the slightest bit while she thinks about her answer. "I think I do. It's not a must. And luckily, my job will let me work wherever I need to, but I'd like to go home for a little while. If only to get Le Désir really producing how we want it to. We were kicking around a few different ideas before I left, and we've got so much to still figure out." She runs a hand over Elodie's back soothingly, and I might be jealous of a baby. "But here's the thing, Coop. We'll figure all that out together. Because I go where you go."

I stand and press a hand to her back, ghosting my lips over hers. "Yeah, baby. We'll figure it out." Because she's wrong. Without the Navy to dictate my next move, I'll be the one following her.

COOPER

Rook and I spend the rest of the day working through the data on the flash drive. Phoenix has someone doing the same thing on their end, but we want to make sure nothing's missed.

I get it. They specialize in shutting down human trafficking.

But Rook and I know Axel.

At least, we thought we did.

I don't think he was a criminal mastermind.

These can't be his offshore accounts. And some of the tracking information on the women who were sold goes back for years. I can't believe he's been involved in this shit for that long.

A feeling scratches at something in my brain.

Him asking about the money. About the five million dollars in the failed op.

Fuck. "Axel talked about the money."

Rook shuts the laptop and stares at me. "Explain."

"We were on the roof, waiting for the exchange, and he asked if I'd ever seen that much money before. I told him I hadn't and that we weren't going to see it then either. And I think he told me I was wrong." I rub my temples. "No. That's not right. That was after."

"After what?" The impatience in Rook's tone pisses me off.

"I'm not sure. This is the first time anything has come

back to me. They're flashes. But I think they're mixed-up. Out of order." I rub my eyes in frustration. But the scratching is gone. "Fuck. It was right there. Like I could reach out and touch it until someone yanked it the hell away."

"Give it time, man. The game's starting in a minute. Why don't we turn it on and watch San Diego kick your friends' asses?" He puts his laptop back in the bag and stretches. We've been at this shit for hours.

"Yeah. Dream on. My brother-in-law could wipe the field with San Diego's quarterback."

"We'll see." Rook grabs the bag and takes it upstairs to the room he's sleeping in, while I move into the living room.

Carys has sketches of lingerie spread across the floor and earbuds in her ears when I step up behind her and drop a kiss to the top of her head. She turns, startled, then pops an earbud from one ear. "Wanna watch your brother and Brady kick San Diego's ass?"

"Ohh. Yes, please." She jumps up from the floor and gathers her sketches as I watch over her shoulder.

The detail is amazing. She's gotten even better since I saw her last sketches. "These are really good, baby. Any chance you want to model some for me later?" I wrap a possessive arm around her waist from behind, and she spins and bats her lashes at me.

"I haven't made these to model yet. And my sewing machine is sitting in Chloe's guest room, missing me." She lifts up on her toes and runs her mouth over my ear. "But I've got something better under my clothes," she whispers in a seductive tone that has my cock springing to life.

"Oh yeah? And what's that?" My hands slide down her back and cup her ass the way I've wanted to since this morning, dragging her body close to mine.

She hums deep in her throat, her warm breath teasing my skin, and whispers, "I'm not wearing anything under my clothes." She nips my ear. "Not a single thing." Then she steps out of my hold and hurries into the kitchen, dropping her sketches on the island and rummaging in the cabinets for snacks for the game.

Leaving me standing in front of the TV with an overwhelming desire to find out if she's telling the truth and an erection that needs adjusting.

When Carys comes back into the room a few minutes later, she's got a big bowl of her favorite pretzels and two bottles of iced tea in her hands. She situates herself next to me on the couch and hands me one of the drinks. "It's not exactly the spread Mom puts out for Coach and Declan's away games, but it'll have to do."

I throw my arm across the back of the couch and run my fingers over her head, massaging it until she moans.

"God, that feels good."

Rook joins us, bitching, "I'm glad you two figured your shit out, but you're not exactly the porn I wanna watch, okay?"

"Ew," Carys giggles. "If that was your idea of porn, I guess I understand why you've been single the entire time I've known you."

He sits down in one of the reclining chairs at the end of the sectional. "That's by choice."

"Ha," she mocks him. "Sure, it is."

Luckily a woman steps onto the field to sing the National Anthem, distracting these two from their bickering. And once the game starts, all eyes are on the TV. Murphy gets a few good tackles, and Brady has no problem scoring on San Diego's defense. By the beginning of the second quarter, the Sentinels are up ten to nothing, and Carys has fallen asleep with her head on my shoulder

163

when Emerson comes downstairs, carrying a baby monitor.

She sits on the opposite end of the couch from Rook, who raises his brow. "Where's the kid?"

Emerson rolls her eyes and grabs the bowl of pretzels. "*My daughter* is asleep in her bassinet." She holds the monitor up and shakes it. "I've got it covered." Then she points to Carys. "Is she feeling okay?" Her shoulders droop slightly, and her voice quiets. "She's been taking care of everything for the past week or so. I don't want her to wear herself down and get sick because of me."

"I think she's just tired." I run my fingers through the silky strands of Carys's hair and realize I haven't even thought about whether she was taking care of herself.

Emerson shakes her head and kicks her legs up on the ottoman. "Have you guys gotten any further with the Axel stuff?"

A warning rings in my head.

Emerson has seemed better the last day or so, but I don't want to be the reason she has a setback.

As if reading my mind, she picks up a pretzel and throws it at my head. "I'm not a problem to be managed, Sinclair." When Rook snorts, she levels him with a glare. "Are you any closer to figuring out what the hell's going on? I don't like living in lockdown. I want to feel the sun on my skin, *and* I want to go back to my own home."

Damn. I feel like shit for not thinking about that.

But in all fairness, this is where Em was already living when I got back to the states.

I just assumed this was where she wanted to be.

"Gonna have to wait a little longer, Em." Rook looks back at the game on TV but keeps talking. "Let's stop there tomorrow after the doctor though. I want to check out your security system anyway. We might need to upgrade you."

"Be careful, Rook. I might start to think you actually like me," she challenges.

"I tolerate you. But you'll always be family, even if you are too damn mouthy." He looks at her out of the corner of his eye as she closes her eyes and laughs.

"I *am* mouthy, aren't I?" Em swings her head to the TV in time to see Brady throw a beautiful spiral down the field. "Is that your brother-in-law?"

"Yeah. That's Brady." It's incredible to see him out on that field. To see Murphy and him on the same damn team. It's the dream they talked about in high school.

"You really are lucky to have such a big family around you. You should take Carys back to Pennsylvania. You guys deserve to be there, surrounded by all the crazy." She grabs the pillow next to her and squeezes it to her chest. "Jack and I always wished we had a big crazy family. Don't throw yours away, Coop." Her eyes shine, but she doesn't cry.

I wish I could take away her pain.

"After we take care of Axel." *Whatever that looks like.* "Then maybe we'll go home." The words feel funny as I say them.

I love Kroydon Hills, but it doesn't feel like home.

But suddenly, neither does San Diego.

Not anymore.

Emerson dips her head in a shaky nod. "After."

CARYS

One of the things I've learned over the past year is to listen to my body. So when I wake up at the end of the game, after having slept through more than half of the action, and still don't feel rested, I know it's time to go to bed. I lift my head from Cooper's shoulder and look around.

"Did we win?"

Rook groans, and a smile stretches across Cooper's face as his arm tightens around me. "Rook's just salty because the Sentinels won. Brady threw a perfect spiral in the fourth quarter that clinched it. There was no coming back after that."

"Whatever," Rook sulks. "The refs sucked. They lost San Diego the game."

I stretch my arms above my head and look around. "I thought Emerson was down here."

"She went upstairs to feed Elodie a while ago." Coop stands, then pulls me up with him. "You hungry?"

Rook grabs the last handful of pretzels from the bowl. "I could eat."

"I wasn't talking to you." Coop walks us into the kitchen, directing me to sit down while he opens the refrigerator. "We had some groceries delivered earlier."

"You gonna cook for me, Coop?" With my elbow on the counter, I rest my chin in my hand and watch him move around the kitchen. "I didn't know you knew how."

Grabbing a plate, Cooper pulls a few steaks from the fridge and some potatoes from a wire bowl on the counter. "I can grill a mean steak. Not exactly cook a four-course dinner. But you need to eat something."

He rounds the corner and drops a kiss on my lips. "There's stuff for a salad in there too. Emerson ordered everything. She said she can't go another day without eating something green."

My eyes stay glued to his ass as he walks out onto the back deck and fires up the grill. Rook brings his empty glass and the pretzel bowl into the kitchen, adding them to the dishwasher, and then turns toward me. I see a question practically on the tip of his tongue, but he's not saying anything.

"What kinds of deep thoughts are you working through over there, soldier?" I move to the other side of the island and lay a few ingredients for a salad on the counter.

"Has he talked to you?" Rook looks toward the door, then back at me.

"About what?" I dump the lettuce in the wooden bowl and start cutting up the tomatoes.

Rook grabs one out of my pile, popping it into his mouth. "Anything? His memory loss? Losing Linc? How fucked up everything is with Axel? He's not talking about it."

"Are you?" I fire back, defensive of Cooper. "Are you guys even allowed to talk about any of that?"

"I'm worried about him, Carys. I talked to my older brother when I first got back to the states. He's always been the one we go to, not that any of us would ever admit it. And if you repeat it, I'll deny every word. But I think Coop needs to talk about it. This shit . . . This life . . . It messes with you. It fucks you up in ways that have nothing to do with the physical. I think, in some ways, Sinclair's using the need to protect you and Em as a reason not to deal with the rest of it." He hands me a cucumber, once I've added the tomatoes to the salad. "I'm worried about the fucker."

I dice the rest of the salad quietly, thinking about everything Rook just laid out before turning around. "I'll work on it. I don't know if he'll listen to me, but I can try."

Emerson walks into the room with Elodie tucked in her arms. "What do I smell?"

"Coop's grilling steaks." I push the salad away and grab four plates from the cabinet.

"Good. My evil plan worked." Her smile stretches a mile wide. "I figured if I ordered enough meat, one of the two men who've decided to live in my house wouldn't be able to help themselves, and you and I would have a dinner we didn't have to make ourselves."

"You're a genius." I kiss the baby's head before I set the table.

"What's that look for, Rook?"

Em points at his face as the man mutters something sounding an awful lot like, "Evil genius."

After I set the table, I pull my phone out and shoot off a text.

Carys: Soooo . . . Something big happened.
Chloe: Well, after today's game, we know Cooper didn't break Murphy.
Daphne: Do we though?
Maddie: Umm, excuse me. Why are we assuming it had to be Cooper who hurt Murphy? Why couldn't Carys have done it herself?
Carys: Thank you, Maddie. Little sisters unite!
Carys: And why are we assuming anyone was maimed

169

here, people? Is it that hard to believe it was a civilized dinner?

Chloe: Civilized and your brother are not two words we put together, Carys.

Carys: Point taken. BUT. But, but, but . . . you're missing MY point.

Daphne: Do you actually have a point?

Carys: We made up.

Maddie: Made what up?

Daphne: OMG, Mads. WTF. You are not that blonde.

Maddie: Oh . . . OH. YAY! That's awesome.

Daphne: I'm so happy you guys worked through your shit.

Chloe: Thank the freaking gods. Now how about you listen to all of us next time when we tell you you're making a mistake?

Carys: No next time. I promise. I'm never letting go again.

Maddie: That's so romantic. I want to fall in love.

Daphne: You wanna get laid, Mads. Love can come after you pop your cherry.

Carys: You guys are crazy.

Chloe: But you love us.

Carys: Damn straight.

I barely finish putting away the dinner dishes when the doorbell rings, and Ford walks thru by himself. "Hey, Ford. No Jessie tonight?" I'm selfishly relieved. I'm exhausted.

"Hey, Carys." He hooks an arm around me and squeezes. "Nope. She picked up a shift at the hospital for a friend."

"Okay. Well, I'm going to bed." I lift up on my toes and kiss Cooper's cheek.

"It's eight o'clock." Emerson looks outside as if to make sure she's right. "And you just woke up a little while ago. Are you feeling okay?"

"I'm fine," I promise. "Just tired and listening to my body. Give me a few hours, and if you need me, I can get up with Elodie after that."

"No. We'll be fine. Go to bed. I'm going to see how she does tonight. Tomorrow is a big day. We get to leave the house, don't we, baby girl?" She smiles down at Elodie in her arms. "We've got the doctor's appointment in the morning, and then I want to stop by the other house. I think I want to move back there before Jack and Theo get home and figure out a way to stop me."

"They mean well, Em." I defend the boys. Knowing how protective they are of her.

"I know. But I'm going to need to do this on my own at some point, and I don't want my brother or anyone else putting their dreams on hold for me." I read between the lines and know I'm the *anyone else* in this scenario.

"Okay. But wake me if you need me." I get a stern look from Em and Coop and decide to make my exit before I press my luck.

I strip out of everything but my shirt, climb into bed, bury my face in a pillow that smells like Cooper, and immediately feel sleep pulling me under.

Strong arms wrap around me during the night, and I hum as my lips press against a very bare chest. "What time is it?"

"Late. Ford just left."

I wrap my body around Cooper's. "Is everything okay?"

"Nothing to worry about tonight." He tucks me under

his chin, and I tangle my legs with his. Wrapping his hand around my throat and resting his thumb over my thrumming pulse possessively, Cooper shifts between my legs, and a thrill dances down my body.

He runs his other hand under my shirt, and he shoves it up over my head. "I love your body, baby."

His thumb brushes over my pebbled nipple, and a tingle pulls deep inside me.

"Coop," I keen, begging for something . . . For anything . . . For everything.

His lips are everywhere as he works his way down my body, worshipping me, until finally his mouth finds my pussy. "I want to taste you, baby."

I look down my body at his blue eyes and crooked grin.

So fucking sexy.

"What are you waiting for?" I spread my legs and drop my knees to the bed.

He spreads my lips, and a chill dances over my skin. My back arches off the bed and my thighs clench around his head when he sucks my clit into his mouth.

I slide my hands through his hair and tug his face closer, and Cooper places a warm, wet kiss against my pussy, then groans and devours me. There's no slow and soft tonight.

Every swipe of his tongue and stroke of those blunt fingers—pushing inside me, stretching me, fucking me—has me clawing at the sheets as butterflies take flight in my stomach.

Strong hands hold my ass and pull me flush against his mouth.

He growls against my sex, and the intensity of the vibrations sends me reeling.

My hips lift, and my body tightens around him. The pressure builds higher and higher, until it's too much and not enough at the same time, entwining around me like a curling ribbon. A knot waiting to be tugged free.

My hands move without thought, tangling in Cooper's hair, tugging him harder, while I shamelessly grind against his face.

I can't hold back the moans slipping past my lips. The begging. The pleading.

My skin burns as the frenzied pleasure builds inside me.

Until it's too much.

Needing to break free, and with one scrape of his finger inside me, hitting a spot only Cooper will ever know, I detonate in a violent orgasm that shakes me to my core as I shatter around him.

COOPER

I KISS THE INSIDE OF CARYS'S THIGH, JUST GETTING STARTED.

She lays still on the bed with a sated and sexy smile on her face.

Like a woman who's just been well fucked, but I have other plans for her.

Kissing and licking every inch of her skin, I enjoy the sounds of Carys's whimpers while she basks in the happy afterglow of her orgasm. I continue dragging out each lash of my tongue against her skin. Grazing my teeth over her hipbones. Pressing a kiss to her taut stomach. I swirl my tongue around her incredible tits and suck each of her pale-pink nipples into my mouth before covering her body with mine.

"I think you broke me," she murmurs against my mouth.

With the taste of her pussy still on my lips, our tongues dance in a slow rhythm.

Tasting.

Exploring.

Remembering.

She mewls against me, bringing her knees up to cradle my hips between her legs. Urging me for more. Silently pleading for me to move.

My cock lays heavy between our legs, the tip teasing her pretty cunt but not pushing in.

Not yet.

I lace my fingers with hers and hold them against the bed on either side of her face while I tease her clit with my dick. Taking my time and rubbing against her soaked core.

"Cooper," she gasps. "Oh God, Coop. I need . . ." Her breath catches in her throat as I inch in slowly, barely moving, before I pull back out.

"What are you doing?" she hisses.

My nose runs down the length of her neck, and my teeth graze her pounding pulse.

"I'm taking my time tonight."

"Cooper . . ." she whines.

"Let me worship you, baby." As if my words break something within her depths, tears leak from the corner of Carys's eyes.

I let go of her hands and try to pull back, but she wraps her arms around my body and holds me to her. "I love you so much, Coop. I'm yours. My body. My heart. My soul." She clings to me like a lifeline. Her lips press against mine until we breathe the same air. "Show me how you love me. Give me you." She wraps a leg around my waist and drags her wet pussy over me. "Give me everything."

Nails scrape up my spine and dig into my shoulder blades as she moves her hips.

I wrap my fingers around her headboard and slowly drive back into her heat as electricity arcs between us. "You were made for me, Carys." I snap my hips, picking up speed.

"Only you, Cooper." She brings her other leg around me, linking them behind my back, her heels digging into the muscles of my ass. "Take me."

My abs contract with each thrust, pulling at my healing scar.

But the pain is exquisite.

It reminds me I'm alive. That I'm here.

That she's not a fucking hallucination I dreamed up because I'm in hell.

"Stay with me, Coop." Carys's hands capture my face, bringing me back to the here and now, and I take her mouth in a bruising kiss.

Our tongues collide, and every hurt, every heartbreak, every fear and doubt we've been carrying falls away.

We move together, drowning in each other.

Clinging to one and other.

"I'm so close, Cooper." She traces my bottom lip with her finger, and I suck it into my mouth, running my tongue around it. Carys's breath falters, and her eyes close. Her inner walls squeeze me like a vise.

Her arm wraps around my neck when she shatters around me, crying out with silent tears pooling in her green eyes.

Pleasure ripples, shooting up from the base of my spine until I follow her over the cliff, filling her. Holding her. Loving her.

The first time I wake up the next morning, it's early. The sun is just peeking over the horizon, and its warm light filters into Carys's room. She's tucked against me. Her hair is a tangled mess, attacking my face, and she's hogging the blanket. But I wouldn't change a single thing.

I adjust my hold on her and close my eyes, deciding this is the only place I have to be.

It takes a minute for my eyes to adjust to the bright room when they open later. Carys is no longer tucked against me. She's sitting against the headboard with her legs crossed and her sketch pad in her hands.

"Good morning." She leans down and kisses me, giving me a glimpse of her sketch.

I pull it from her hands. "Carys Murphy, are you sketching me?" It's not as good as her lingerie sketches, but it's pretty damn obvious it's me.

"Don't let it go to your head, Coop. You're pretty when you sleep." She steals the book back and lays it on her nightstand. "Are you hungry? I was going to go down and make breakfast, but the house was still quiet, and I didn't want to wake anyone up."

I drag her down by her legs and cage her in against the mattress. "Is that what you really want?"

Carys giggles, then tickles my sides until I let her go. "What I want is to eat something semi-healthy before lacing up my sneakers and going for a run. I haven't run once in the past week, and I need to, Coop. Please tell me you'll come with me and let me get some sun, fresh air, and non-sex-induced endorphins . . . *please.*"

I think about how Rook's brothers reported there was still no sign of Axel as of last night during our Zoom call.

Ford, Rook, and I went over everything we know, as well as every idea we had, and still came up with a big fat fucking goose egg at the end of it.

It's infuriating that someone we've trained side by side with would be the guy we're chasing because he knows everything we do.

He knows how to hide.

How to cover his tracks.

How to be invisible.

But that also means, if there's a strike coming, it's not going to happen in public.

"Fine," I give in. "But I'm coming with you, and we're running on the beach." I don't tell her that's safest because there's nowhere to hide. Instead, I throw the covers off and get out of bed.

"Where are you going?" She sits up with a pout.

I pick her up in a firemen's hold and smack a hand against her bare ass.

"Cooper . . ." she squeals. "What are you doing?"

"We need a shower," I tell her before stepping into the bathroom.

"We're going to get dirty again, Coop." This beautiful woman smiles as she slides down my body, and a wicked grin crosses my face.

"I know."

CARYS

Lacing up my running shoes is like putting on that one pair of jeans everyone has. The pair that makes your ass look fantastic and puts a smile on your face. Running is like that for me. Yes, it does help my ass look better—not quite fantastic, but good enough.

But it's how it makes me feel that's addictive. And staying active, eating right, and taking care of my body and my mental health are all supposed to help prevent flare-ups. Not completely—because nothing will ever do that. But the better care I take of myself, the better off I'll be.

Mom found me an incredible doctor in Philly who I met with over the summer, and I really liked her. She talked to me about everything, not just about my lupus. We talked about things I could do that would help me feel better overall. Ways to prevent flare-ups, not just ways to treat them once they happened. "Shit."

"What's wrong?" Cooper moves up behind me, and I turn, seeing he's in basketball shorts and an old t-shirt that stretches tight across his chest and around his biceps. His Kings ball cap is on backward, holding back his hair and making the whole package utterly irresistible. "My eyes are up here, Miss Murphy." The ass uses my own words against me.

"Shut up." I tie my other shoe, then stand. "I have a doctor's appointment scheduled in Kroydon Hills next week. I forgot about it. I guess I should cancel it."

"No. You shouldn't, Carys. You need to go to that appointment," he pushes.

I slide my phone into the pocket of my leggings. "Kinda on the wrong side of the country, Coop."

"Then go home, Carys. Your health is just as important as Emerson's." His hand tugs on my ponytail and tilts my head back toward his. "Go home for a few days. You can always come back if you want. Emerson wouldn't want you to miss it."

I push him away and walk outside. "You act like it's a car ride away. It's eight hours on a plane. Not exactly a weekend trip."

Coop follows me out and locks the door. The two of us stretch, and his eyes are glued to my ass the entire time. *Another benefit of running.*

"Just think about it. Please."

I bend over and place my palms flat on the deck, deliberately placing my ass in front of his face and hoping to distract him. But he smacks it instead, sending a jolt to my core.

"Don't be a brat, Carys. That's not playing fair." He jogs down the steps, and I follow behind him.

"I'll make you a deal . . ."

Cooper turns back to me, brow raised. "Lay it on me. What's your deal?"

"I'll figure out a way to go to my appointment—including virtual, if that's an option—*if* you'll make an appointment to talk to someone." His happy expression is wiped blank, and he stares at me.

"Have you been talking to Rook?" He's masking his frustration well, but I still see it.

I step up to him and lace my fingers through his. "You need to talk to someone, Coop. There's so much going on . . ."

"And I will. When this is all over and I have five minutes to deal with everything else. Keeping you safe and finding Axel are the only two things I can worry about right now, Carys. They're the only things that matter." He tries to drop my hand, but I refuse to let him.

"Tough shit, Sinclair. You matter. Your health matters. I don't get to be your excuse for not healing. You're not dealing with it. You're pushing it aside." I pull his hand up to my face and rub it against my cheek. "Do it for me if you won't do it for yourself."

"That's playing dirty, mini-Murphy." He cracks a reluctant smile.

I run my finger along his bottom lip. "Did it work?"

He wraps his arms around me and presses his lips to my forehead. "Yeah, it worked. I'll call. But I'm not promising anything else yet, okay?"

I rise up on my toes and run my lips over his. "Thank you. Now, are you ready to get your ass handed to you by a girl?"

"Dream on, baby."

I pop my earbuds in and point to my ears. "I can't hear you." Then I take off. Cooper catches up to me with ease, and we find a comfortable rhythm for our five-mile run.

Running on the beach always slows me down, but Cooper was a champ and didn't complain even though I could tell my twelve-minute mile was a little slow for him. When I press my palms to the outside wall of the house and stretch out my legs, he crowds my body from behind.

"Do you have any idea what watching your ass in those pants for the past hour has done to me?" He presses his erection against my ass, and my mind runs wild with the possibilities.

"I think I have an idea." I spin in his arms, and he lifts me from my feet. "But I'm always happy for a demonstration. I don't think I realized just how much of an ass man you are."

"I'm a *you* man, Carys." Cooper carries me into the house and takes the stairs two at a time as he gets us to my room in record time.

My hot skin prickles with awareness as we step through the door, and Coop sets me back on my feet.

He moves in front of me, blocking me.

"Stay here," he demands, and every muscle in his body is strung tight and on alert.

I take a step back as an uneasy feeling blankets my skin. "What's wrong?"

"The balcony door wasn't shut" is whispered in my ear, sending a jolt of fear straight through me.

Oh, God. *Axel.*

A gun presses against my temple.

My eyes dart to Cooper's in the reflection of the glass door across the room, and I begin shaking uncontrollably. Fear coats my skin and sends my thoughts racing. I'm not ready to die.

Coop turns, pulling his gun out of his duffle on the dresser as he spins around.

His blue eyes assess the situation in seconds.

And I'm suddenly less worried for myself and more worried for him.

"I warned you, Sinclair," Axel sneers, pulling my body in front of his. "I told you I'd take something of yours if you didn't give me back what's mine. I gave you a fucking out. Just give me the flash drive, and this all ends."

Tears pool in my eyes, and my heart rate spikes out of control as fear paralyzes me. "Axel, please," I cry.

"Don't." He jerks me back, and my tears flow down my face. "This isn't my fault. It's your boy's over there." He presses the gun tighter against my head, hurting me.

Cooper steps forward, completely calm except for the fury I see in his eyes.

"Don't fucking move." Axel shakes as he screams across my room.

"Leave her out of this, Axe. This is between us." Cooper points his gun at Axe, but Axel angles behind me.

My legs feel like they're going to give out beneath me.

Oh God, I'm a human shield.

I'm not ready to die. Not ready to lose Coop's life or mine.

"She's got nothing to do with this, Axe." Cooper's voice is casual, like he's not bargaining for our lives. "Let her go. We can work it out between us."

"I. Need. The. Flash drive," Axel roars, and I tremble, not sure how I'm still standing. "My life means nothing without it. Give it to me, and I leave. Give it to me, and this ends. We all walk away."

Cooper's shoulders drop, deflating. I pray Axel doesn't see the tiny difference in him. "I don't have it."

Oh, God. No.

"What the fuck do you mean you don't have it?" Axel explodes as he wraps an arm tightly across my chest. "Where is it?"

Cooper's trying to reason with him, but I think Axel's past the point of reasoning.

The gun presses even tighter against my skull, and I wince in pain.

Blood pounds in my ears, and my body shakes as silent tears continue to fall.

At least he knows I love him.

"It's a few hours north of here. One of Rook's brothers has it. Take me. I'll bring you to him. We'll go get it together. Just leave her out of this." Cooper inches forward, continuing to remain calm even as Axel's composure breaks.

"No, Cooper." My heart pounds out of my chest. I refuse to trade his life for mine and let him get in the car with this killer. I refuse to let him die. "Don't leave."

Cooper's eyes flare with anger and apprehension.

"Listen to your girl, Sinclair. She's smarter than you. I'm not about to let you walk me into a trap." Axel's shaking hand rubs against my body, and I freeze. "Fuck. Fuck! This wasn't supposed to happen. None of this was supposed to happen this way."

Cooper's eyes grow wide with Axel's words, and all the regret of this past year drowns me when I realize this could be it . . .

COOPER

Axel's words trigger my memory, and it comes back to me like a flash-bang.

"Disable the last car" is ordered. I don't hesitate before taking out their tires.

"Are we taking out the others?" I ask, then look over at Axel, who's been strangely quiet. "Axe, man. You with me?"

He doesn't answer right away.

"Axel," I yell. "You okay, brother?"

"Fuck. Fuck! This wasn't supposed to happen." Axel isn't making any sense. "Fuck, Linc. Let her go."

Ford is fighting a losing battle on the ground, trying to calm everyone down when the first gunshot is fired from the terrorists' second vehicle.

Linc secures Saylor and takes cover to return fire. Our team is in a standoff, and Axe and I are supposed to be covering them.

Out of the corner of my eye, I see Linc go down. But the angle of the shot . . . it's wrong.

I shift to look at Axel.

He's already on his feet, coming my way.

His rifle is on the rooftop, and his handgun is pointed at me.

"What did you do?" I look up at him from my position, not believing what I just saw.

A small electronic device falls from his pocket, and I grab it, shoving it in mine.

"I'm gonna need you to give that back to me, Sinclair." Axe

points his gun at my head, and I sweep my leg out and up, taking him down at the ankles. He falls backward and pulls his trigger.

Red-hot heat tears through my body a second before the building collapses.

Nobody warned me what it's like to look back with regret.

To be left wondering, *What if . . . ?*

What if I'd told her sooner?

What if I hadn't missed the signs?

It was my job to protect them . . . What if I hadn't failed?

What if I'd only had a little more time?

Axel stands across from me. His shaking hand is holding a gun pressed to Carys's temple, and I can't make a move. At no point during my training has anything ever prepared me for having her life in the hands of a highly trained, desperate killer.

Her lips tremble in fear, and I have no way to comfort her.

No good shot to take him out without risking her life.

"None of this was supposed to happen. It was supposed to be easy money. Help them get the money and keep the girls. That's what my contact said. That's what they wanted." Axel shields himself with Carys in front of him.

He anticipates every move I make.

He can predict my actions the way I'm positive of his reactions.

He knows I won't risk her.

But with each passing second, he's becoming more agitated.

More unstable.

It's my only play. Unstable can mean sloppy. And sloppy can offer an opportunity.

"What about Linc? If nobody was supposed to get hurt, why is Linc dead?" The words hide my hate. They're calm, masking my fury.

As long as he's talking, there's a chance I can get us out of this.

"This isn't you, man. You don't betray your team." I inch forward again. "Your brothers."

"You're not my brother, Sinclair. You've got a rich brother and a richer daddy who can take care of you. I ain't got shit to go home to. This was my score. Help them out on one op and get a million-dollar payday. They approached me in the city before our team ever knew about the mission. They knew. They'd been planning. Easy money, they said. But nothing's ever easy, so before the guy left the café that day, I swiped the flash drive from the pocket of his briefcase. An insurance policy." He shakes his head, lost in the thought.

Remorse is written over every inch of his face, but it's too late for that.

He and I both know it.

We're not both getting out of here alive.

"Dumb fuck. He didn't even notice. Not then. And when I got back to base and saw what was on it . . . That wasn't just a million-dollar payday. The contents of that little flash drive were going to set me up for life. They weren't even encrypted."

My reaction must flash across my face because he raises a brow.

"Your boys haven't been able to crack it, have they? I encrypted that shit myself. Couldn't have anybody stumble onto what's on there. I figured, after I got my million, I'd tell them what I found and offer them a way to buy it back.

Then I'd live out the rest of my life sipping margaritas out of a coconut on a beach somewhere in South America."

Axel jerks his arm back and catches Carys's jaw, causing her to cry out, but it doesn't even register with him.

"If no one was supposed to get hurt . . . if everything was easy, what the fucking hell happened, man?" *Keep him talking* plays over and over in my mind.

A mantra I'm fighting for.

Praying it works.

"They figured out I had it. One of their guys made contact the morning of the op. Told me if I didn't hand it over and make sure they left with the money and both girls, I was dead. Once I explained there were already copies and it wouldn't be that easy to silence me, we struck a deal we could both walk away from."

My eyes stay locked on Carys's, but she's panicking. Her eyes are glazed and unfocused, and I can see from here her breathing is shallow and rapid.

I see it but can't stop it.

Fuck.

"Carys." Her green eyes snap to mine, centering on me.

"Don't talk to her. Do you want to wear her brains, Sinclair? I got nothing to lose, so don't make me pull this trigger."

Her body shakes as she tries to breathe through her fear.

"I still don't get it. Why Linc?" My brain is scrambling for a way to disarm him without him killing her, but the risks are too high.

"He got to Saylor." His wild eyes bounce around the room, probably finalizing his exit strategy. "I needed both girls to leave with the group, not with our team. They couldn't be saved. That was part of the deal. And there was no way Linc was letting her go. It was his life or mine." The gun moves, pushing harder against Carys's pale skin, and I know I'll never forget the terror in her eyes. "Kinda like now. I'm not gonna die today, Sinclair. So you can ignore your savior complex. Me and baby momma are gonna walk out of here, and you're gonna let us."

"No," Carys cries out, and Axe presses his forearm to the front of her neck. "Cooper . . ." she sobs.

"We're gonna back through this door, and you're gonna let me, or she's gonna die. I got nothing left to lose, Sinclair. You better believe if her life is my only bargaining chip, I'm gonna play it."

Carys's cell phone rings in the pocket of her leggings.

It's not much, but it's enough.

I take the shot.

Red blooms directly between his eyes, and I dive for Carys, hoping to God his finger doesn't squeeze the trigger as we go down.

CARYS

OH, GOD." MY PHONE VIBRATES ONCE FROM THE POCKET OF my leggings.

Then the obnoxious ringtone Chloe programmed for herself pierces the silence. Everything happens within a split-second after that. But it feels like slow-motion.

A powerful boom discharges.

A flash hits me from the other side of the room.

I'm knocked down, and my head crashes into the corner of my bed before I hit the ground. "Cooper," I cry. "Oh, God. Coop . . ."

"I've got you, baby. Don't look." He cradles my body to his, covering me. "Are you okay?"

"I don't . . . I'm not . . ." Words are hard to form as my vision begins to narrow. "My head hurts."

He pulls his hand away, and blood covers his fingers. "Oh shit, Carys. Don't close your eyes."

"Are you okay?" I whisper. Terrified.

"I'm fine, baby, and so are you," his voice cracks.

But I don't think he's right because my heavy lids refuse to stay open. "Love you, Coop."

"Don't go to sleep, baby. Please don't leave me."

He sounds so far away.

When I wake up, my body is strapped to a board, and an unfamiliar face is above me. "Who are you?" I ask weakly.

Flashes of what happened in my bedroom assault me, and tears stream down the sides of my face. "Where's Cooper?" I ask the man in a paramedic's uniform. "Oh, God." I look around. "Am I in an ambulance? I need Cooper."

A hand squeezes mine before the stranger can answer. "We're on our way to the hospital, Carys." Rook's voice is calm with an edge of authority. "You hit your head. Probably just a concussion, but you need a few stitches. No big deal."

"Where's Cooper?" I try to lift my head, but it's strapped down. And a new round of fear coats my skin. "Where is he?"

"He's fine. The police are at the house, and Ford's with him. Emerson and I pulled up at the same time the cops did." He moves my hair away from my face, more gently than I thought Rook was capable of. "Trust me when I say Cooper will be at the hospital as soon as possible. I thought he was gonna get himself arrested when they told him he couldn't come with you."

I don't realize I'm still crying until Rook wipes my tears from my cheeks. "It's over, Carys. Cooper ended it. He did what had to be done."

He killed someone.

In. My. Bedroom.

My stomach revolts. "I'm going to be sick."

I close my eyes and breathe in through my nose and out through my mouth, steadying my breath and my stomach until we get to the hospital.

Every part of me hurts as they wheel me through the doors of the emergency room.

My head, my eyes, my body. It all aches, and I just want Cooper here, holding my hand.

"There's our girl." Jessie moves to my side, opposite Rook, when I'm wheeled in past a desk. She might as well be speaking another language while she and the paramedic discuss my status.

Once I'm moved to a bed behind a curtain, Jessie and another nurse check me over before a doctor comes in and does the same thing.

Once the doctor steps up next to me, Jess fills him in, kisses my cheek, and tells me she'll be back to check on me as soon as she can.

Rook holds my hand while the doctor numbs my head with a disturbingly large needle, and my stomach somersaults again.

It takes six stitches to close the gash at the base of my skull before they can take me for a CAT scan. Rook stays by my side until they tell him he can't go past a certain point.

"Can you call Cooper, please?" I plead. "Make sure he's okay?"

He nods and leans against the wall of the hallway. "I'll be right here until they wheel you out."

"Promise?" I can't believe how needy I am.

But it hasn't all sunken in yet, and I keep reliving it.

I still feel the cool metal of the gun pressed against my temple.

The smell of his rancid breath every time it ghosted across my face.

The look in Cooper's eyes as he silently pleaded with me to stay strong.

Rook lifts his brow. "Never doubt a SEAL, Carys. We'll prove you wrong every single time. Your boy's gonna be fine, and so are you. Now go get your cat scanned." He crosses his legs at his ankles and pulls his phone from his pocket.

"Sir," the nurse scolds. "You can't use that here."

Rook glares until she looks away, muttering about entitled assholes, and wheels me through the door.

What feels like a lifetime later, but is probably only an hour, the curtain surrounding my bed in the emergency room is pulled back, and the doctor from earlier moves next to me. He glances at Rook briefly. "Would you excuse us, sir?"

"You've got zero chance of me leaving her side, doc. So, you might as well get on with it." He kicks his legs up against the wheels of the bed and leans back, getting himself comfortable. If it wouldn't make my brain hurt, I might have even laughed.

"How are you feeling, Ms. Murphy?" He looks one more time at Rook, then takes a step away from the bed.

Like I was just attacked by a crazy fucking sociopath, then watched the love of my life kill him, doesn't seem to be an appropriate answer. So instead, I go with, "Like I hit my head."

"How many fingers am I holding up?" He places his hand in front of me at the foot of my bed.

"Four fingers." I'm already growing irrationally tired of this.

"And do you know where you are?" He side-eyes Rook, who grunts, and I swear this doctor has to think Rook is a threat from the way he's reacting to him.

I guess, in a way he is, while Rook is playing the part of my bodyguard.

"I'm in San Diego, California. I'd tell you today's date if I knew it, but my best friend had a baby last week, and I'm not actually sure of the date. October something. Fifth, sixth, seventh? Something like that. It's Monday. My name is Carys Murphy. The man being a pain in the ass is Rook . . ." I look at him and tilt my head. "What the hell is your last name, soldier boy?"

"She's being sarcastic, doc. I think she's fine."

The doctor looks between us and shakes his head. "You have a concussion, Ms. Murphy. But there's nothing leading me to believe you need to stay in the hospital. The good news is you only lost consciousness once. The rest of your symptoms seem to be mild. So, I want you to go home and rest, *if* and only *if*," he looks hesitantly at Rook, "you will have someone there with you."

The curtain is pulled back, and Cooper darts to my side, blood spatter still covering his shirt. He wraps his arms around me, and I sob uncontrollably.

Relief, fear, and grief all pouring out at once.

I'm vaguely aware of Rook answering the doctor. "She's got someone. How about we get those discharge papers now, doc?"

COOPER

I press my lips to her forehead and hold Carys close to me while she cries, ignoring everyone around us. Lost in the relief that she's here. She's alive and clinging to me, like I didn't just shoot someone in front of her. "Shh. It's okay. We're okay."

"Are we?" she asks between ragged breaths. "Are you okay? What did the police say? What did the Navy say?" She clings to me, and I finally feel like I can breathe again.

"It was self-defense. I'm not under arrest. Ford is dealing with the Navy." The local police made me go over everything with three different detectives more times than I can count before the military police showed up. They still have jurisdiction since Axel was a Navy SEAL. Even if he was AWOL. Ford smoothed things over with them so I could get to Carys as soon as possible.

Holding her in my arms with her blood *literally* on my hands as she passed out was the scariest fucking moment of my life.

Now, as I sit next to her, she lays her head on my chest, and I refuse to let go. I glance over at Rook and nod. "Thank you for being here when I couldn't."

"Any time, brother. Do you want me to stick around?" Rook shoves his hands in his pockets and looks at my girl with soft, concerned eyes.

"No. I appreciate it. I'm going to take her back to

Trick's house for the night." Carys pulls back and tips her head up to mine.

"For the night? I don't want to go back to the house tomorrow. I don't want to see that room again. Ever." What little color she has drains from her cheeks. "Where's Emerson? Where did she go with Elodie?" Her eyes grow worried. "Oh, God. Did she see . . . ? Was Elodie there?"

"Don't worry about it, I offered her Trick's house, but she said no. I don't think she wanted to be in Linc's room." In reality, she freaked the fuck out, but Carys doesn't need to know that now. I think if I'd taken Elodie from Emerson's arms and handed her my gun, she'd have gone upstairs and shot Axel again. "Ford took her back to her house. She said she was there with Rook earlier, and she threw together a bag to take with her."

"Should we go there? What if she needs help?" My beautiful girl has a heart of gold, but this time, I'm making sure she thinks of herself first for a change.

"No," I shut her down. "We're going to Trick's house tonight, and then we're getting on a plane tomorrow and going back to Kroydon Hills. I've already spoken to Dad and Katherine. It was the only way to convince them not to fly out here." I press my lips to her head. "And I've got to tell you, I really don't want them here."

She opens her mouth to argue, but I gently press my lips to hers. "I love you. Let me take care of you. Please, baby."

With a gentle nod of her head, she whispers, "Fine. Let's go home."

She's quiet for the better part of the next hour, listening to the instructions from her doctor and signing away her life on the discharge papers. It's not until we get in the Jeep that Carys laces her fingers through mine and begins to crash after her adrenaline rush, slumping against the seat.

"You okay?" I squeeze her hand as we pull out of the hospital parking garage. "Want me to stop and get you anything?"

"No. I just want . . . I'm not even sure what I want at this point, Cooper. To sleep for a month, maybe . . . How are *you*?"

"I'm fine." I don't even sound convincing to my own ears. When Carys's eyes bore into the side of my head, I glance her way. Guess I'm not fooling her either. "I'll be fine."

Maybe if we both say it enough, we'll start believing it.

Cooper: Just got home from the hospital. Carys has six stitches and a concussion. We're staying at Trick's tonight.
Dad: Calling now. Answer your phone.

My phone rings with an incoming FaceTime from my dad, and I swipe to answer the call. "Max already has the jet heading to you. It's all over the news, son. Daphne saw it. Everyone's seen it, and everyone's worried sick. How are you both doing? The news said Carys lost consciousness."

"I want to talk to Carys," Katherine demands. "Where is she?"

"She's in the shower right now. But she should be out soon," I tell my stepmother, trying to hide the exhaustion and fear currently fighting for control within me. "We don't need the Kingston jet, Dad. We're going to see if we can get tickets to fly home tomorrow, or Wednesday at the latest." I try to hide my growing frustration at being handled after the fucking day we've had, but I'm doing a piss-poor job of it.

Carys walks out of the bathroom with a towel wrapped around her damp skin and sits down on my lap. Her hands circle my waist, and her head rests on my shoulder.

"Oh, sweetheart." Katherine's hand flies to her mouth. "Thank God you're both okay." Her red eyes well with tears. "When Cooper called . . . We're just so lucky you're both alive and in one piece."

Dad's eyes soften when he sees Carys. "Hey, kiddo. How are you feeling?"

"I'm okay, Coach," she lies. "Just a headache."

"I was just telling Cooper that Max and Daphne insisted they send the jet for you. I think Daphne wanted to come herself, but Max convinced her you both might want a little space." I'll have to remember to thank Max.

"What time will the jet be here?" Carys yawns.

"Not until after midnight. Just let Max know what time you want to leave tomorrow." Dad wraps an arm around a teary Katherine. "We love you kids."

"Love you too, Dad. We'll see you tomorrow." I slide my finger across the screen and end the call, then put the phone down and wrap my arms around Carys.

"You okay?"

"I'm fine, Cooper." She holds my face in her hands. "Physically, I'm fine. My head's going to hurt for a few days. But I'm more worried about *you*. Talk to me. Tell me how you're feeling. And don't tell me you're fine. You killed a man today, Coop."

"And I'd do it again if it meant saving your life, Carys. He's not the first man I've killed." I wrap an arm under her legs and another around her back, then stand and carry her into my room, placing her in the middle of the bed. "I'm going to jump in the shower. Why don't you decide what you want to order for dinner? The fridge is empty, and you need to eat something."

"I'm not hungry." She purses her lips, clearly annoyed with my avoidance.

"Fine. Are you going to call Emerson?" I strip down to my boxers and wait her out.

She stands from the bed and rifles through my closet until she finds the tee she wants and slips it over her head. "I will. I want to see her before we go home tomorrow. I feel like I'm abandoning her."

"You're not abandoning her. You're taking care of your-self." I pick her phone up from the dresser and hold it out for her. "Call her. We can go see her tonight or tomorrow morning. Your choice."

She crosses the room and presses her lips to mine. "I love you, Coop."

"You are the air I breathe, Carys."

CARYS

I STEP OUTSIDE INTO THE BACKYARD, THE GUILT OVER MY conversation with Emerson eating me alive. "Are you sure you won't hate me? I feel terrible leaving early. You've still got another week before Jack and Theo get back." Elodie's fussing in Emerson's arms as Em and I FaceTime.

"I love you, CC. You need to focus on you and Cooper now." She adjusts the baby and drops the phone. "Shit." She grabs it and holds it in front of her again, and I watch Elodie grabbing at Em's top. "Believe it or not, my mom saw the shooting on the news and called to say she was coming to stay with me for a bit. Didn't even give me a chance to tell her no. I think it's the first time in ten years she's actually wanted to act like a mother. She even sounded excited to meet Elodie."

Em murmurs something softly to Elodie and offers her favorite binky.

Which Elodie promptly spits out. She stops fussing long enough to scrunch up her adorable little lips and wail at the top of her not so little lungs. "Sorry, CC. I need to give this baby a boob, or she's going to grow horns and a tail and stab me with a pitchfork. Take care of Cooper, okay? Elodie and I will come see you in Kroydon Hills soon." Then she chokes up. "I wouldn't have gotten through the past few weeks without you, babe."

"Love you, Em. Kiss that baby for me." I choke back my tears, so incredibly tired of crying. "I'll see you soon."

We hang up, and I stare at my phone.

I've missed calls from everyone. Aiden, Nattie, Declan, Chloe, Daphne, and Maddie. I've even had calls from numbers I don't recognize.

My voicemail box is full.

I'm sure Mom and Coach will fill the family in, so I drop down onto the outdoor sectional and pull my knees up to my chest to text the girls.

Carys: Sorry for not calling you all. Coop and I are exhausted, but we're okay.

Chloe: Don't apologize.

Daphne: You're coming home tomorrow, right?

Carys: Yeah. We'll be home sometime tomorrow afternoon. Can you tell Max thank you for sending the jet? He didn't have to do that.

Daphne: Yes, he did, if he ever wanted to sleep next to me again. I'd be on it now if he didn't convince me that you might want some space.

Maddie: Do you need anything?

Carys: Yeah. A place to stay that isn't a few rooms down from our parents.

Maddie: You could always move in with me and my brother now that D moved out.

Daphne: I have a better idea. Hudson just bought some property at Kroydon Falls. It has three houses on adjoining properties. He's been rehabbing the one he's going to live in.

Chloe: Hudson Kingston is knocking down walls with his bare hands? Where can I watch this happening? That's got to be better than porn.

Daphne: Ew. It's more like he's paying someone to do it for him.

Maddie: I second Chloe. That's got to be better than porn.

Carys: I miss you guys!

Daphne: Anyhoo, there's nothing wrong with the other two houses. He just hasn't decided if he wants to sell or rent them out. I can ask him if you could rent one while you're figuring out what you're doing.

Carys: That would be perfect, D. Would you mind checking with Hudson?

Chloe: You know your room here is still yours, right?

Carys: I do, and I love you for it! I just think we might need some space to ourselves when we get home.

Chloe: Fine. I guess that makes sense.

Carys: I'll message when we get home tomorrow.

It's hard to be in this yard and not think about the times we all spent here. Trick and Wanda by the grill. Linc and Em holed up in his room. Ford in the ocean on his surfboard. And Axel torturing me about our nonexistent future children. It feels like a lifetime ago and yesterday, all at once.

Cooper calls out my name, like he's being chased by the hounds of hell.

I don't take two steps before he flies through the back door, terrified, and wraps his arms around me. "Jesus. I didn't know where you were."

This man. This stubborn man, who swears he's okay, buries his face in my hair and runs his hands over my body, like he's making sure I'm real. Making sure I'm whole. This incredible, strong, amazing man, who I love more than anything in this world, doesn't realize just how hard the crash is going to be when everything that happened today hits him and he finally processes that.

The thoughts choke the breath from my body as realization dawns.

When I was faced with dealing with an overwhelming trauma, I pushed him away.

I tighten my hold on his back and kiss his neck.

"I'm right here, Coop. I'm safe. And I'm not going anywhere."

COOPER

IT TAKES WAY TOO LONG FOR MY HEART TO SLOW DOWN
after not being able to find Carys.

Part of me recognizes my reaction was over-the-top.

The rest of me doesn't give a shit after the day
we've had.

We order sandwiches, which neither of us touch, and
watch TV in bed while we continue fielding calls from
everyone. Her brother. My sister and brother. Ford and
Jessie. Bash. Everyone wants to check in. Most of them we
promise to see soon. Ford and Jessie plan to meet us for
coffee at the shop down the street in the morning before
we leave.

The house is a crime scene and taped off for now. But
whenever we can get in again, they agree to grab our
things and send them back to Pennsylvania for us.

The only things I was able to take with me today were
my wallet and her purse.

At least we have our ID's.

Carys stands up and stretches after the closing credits
and bonus scene roll for the movie we put on earlier and
walks toward the door.

"Where are you going?" I ask as my heart races at the
idea of her being out of my sight.

She tilts her head and squints her eyes, like my question
doesn't make sense. "To the bathroom. I'll be right back.
Go ahead and pick the next movie."

My shirt swallows her delicate body, hitting her mid-thigh, and the socks she swiped from my drawer sit sexy on her legs, hitting mid-calf. It shouldn't be a good look, but it looks fantastic on her.

She climbs back into bed a few minutes later with a bottle of ibuprofen and swallows two pills, then curls her body around mine and gets comfy.

"What do you want to watch?" I ask as I scroll through our options.

She hums in the back of her throat. "Anything. I don't care." She pulls the blanket up around us. "I'm falling asleep." She kisses my chin. "Today was too close, Coop. I could have lost you."

"Baby, I had to stand there while someone had a gun to your head. Never again, Carys. I don't want this world touching you ever again." She'll never realize how close we came. I hope she doesn't because it's going to haunt me.

At some point, after having binged basically every movie Adam Sandler has put out this century, I slip out of bed without waking Carys and make sure the doors are locked and the alarm is armed. I don't bother turning the TV off because I don't think I'll be getting much sleep tonight. Not with the visions of the day constantly assaulting me. Only now, they're mixing with my buried memories from the last op.

I was better off before.

When I couldn't remember taking out the enemy's tires.

When I didn't know that my orders . . . that my action was what started the gunfire that led to the chaos. You can't always pinpoint when an op goes sideways. But I now know taking out the enemy's tires was when the gunfire erupted. And while I was concerned with the enemy on the ground, I wasn't protecting our guys from the enemy next to me.

When I didn't remember what happened, at least I wasn't forced to watch it over and over again.

My brain didn't play tricks on me by replacing Linc's face with Carys's.

When the alarm goes off in the morning, letting us know it's time to get moving if we want to catch up with Ford and Jessie, I'm not sure I've managed to even get a solid hour of sleep.

I lay in bed all night, holding her. Watching her. Feeling her heart beat against my chest.

"Time to wake up, sleeping beauty." I press my lips to hers, and she wraps herself around me.

Carys groans. "What time is it?" Her emerald-green eyes flutter open, then she squints and closes them again. "Why is it so bright?"

"It's time to get dressed, if we're going to meet Ford and Jess for coffee." I run my hand along the curves of her body. "How are you feeling?"

"My head hurts a little, and my muscles feel like I ran a marathon." Carys curls into me, wrapping herself around me. She lays her hand over my heart. "How are you feeling? Did you get any sleep last night?"

"I'm fine. Your muscles are sore from the adrenaline dump. You didn't feel anything yesterday because the adrenaline protected you from it. It's always worse the next day." I throw the blanket off us and climb out of bed. "Now, move that sweet ass. We've got to get going."

"Coop . . ." My stomach drops as she sits up and looks at me with concern in her eyes. "Talk to me. Neither of us should be fine today." When she climbs out of bed, it's with slow and cautious movements, accentuating how sore her body must be.

My palms run up her arms. "Come here, baby." I tuck her against my chest and breathe her in, calming my demons. "Everything is going to be alright. Don't worry about me. I was trained for this."

She wraps her arms around my waist and presses her lips to my chest. "I hope you're right."

We stand there in the quiet room for another minute before I smack her butt. "Okay, baby, you've got to move that sweet ass, if we're going to get to the coffee shop on time."

Carys laughs and shakes her ass. "It's moving a little slower right now. I need some medicine and some caffeine. Not necessarily in that order. Oh, and I guess clothes, since mine are all part of a crime scene now." She searches through my drawer until she finds a pair of old sweats and rolls them over at the waist a few times. Then she pulls on a Navy tee while slipping into her sneakers.

I get dressed quickly and stuff some of my things into a carry-on. Then I stop and look around the room.

"Are you going to miss it?" Concern laces her voice.

"I'm going to miss all of it. The place. The guys. My career. But it's time. No point in putting it off." Without the team . . . and without my job, my purpose . . . This isn't where I'm supposed to be anymore. I tug her behind me.

Carys looks up at me with sparkling eyes. "You ready to go home?"

"You are my home, Carys."

CARYS

I USED TO THINK MY LIFE WAS BORING.

I prayed for some excitement.

To be noticed. To be included. To be loved.

I've decided excitement is overrated.

I still want that love that sets the city on fire . . . and I've got it. He's asleep next to me on the Kingston jet as the attendant announces we're only twenty minutes out from Philadelphia. He's my real-life knight in shining armor. The man my heart beats for . . . lives for. And he's hurting.

I think I should be more traumatized by what happened yesterday, but it hasn't set in yet. I have every intention of reaching out to a therapist once we get settled so I can work through the whole thing. I refuse to let Axel be a defining moment in my life. He doesn't deserve that. But I'm worried about Cooper.

I slept like shit last night. Tossing and turning all night. And every time I opened my eyes, Cooper was still awake. I'm not sure if he slept at all until the jet took off. He crashed hard then and has been asleep ever since.

I can't imagine what this is doing to him. And I'm scared he's going to bottle it up until he explodes.

Even in his sleep, he reaches for me now. As if to make sure I'm still here.

He looks peaceful.

Relaxed.

And I realize I haven't seen him relaxed or at ease in months.

Not since before I tore his heart out.

I lean against him and skim my mouth over the shell of his ear. "We're almost home, Coop."

He turns his head and captures my lips in a soul-stealing kiss.

Strong hands slide up my arms and drag me against his chest. His tongue licks my lips, begging for entrance, and I sigh happily and suck it into my mouth, clutching him to me until we're both gasping for breath. We're interrupted when the attendant comes over the speaker, announcing our descent.

"To be continued," I tease.

He presses his thumb against my lip, and I nip at it. "When are we looking at the house on the lake? The things I want to do to you require a level of privacy we won't get at Dad and Katherine's."

As if a bucket of ice water was just thrown over my head, I back up into my own seat and pout. "Not soon enough. Daphne told me to text her when we get up tomorrow, and we can meet her there after that. It's going to be too late by the time we land tonight."

He grabs my hand and places it over his hard dick, pressing against the zipper of his jeans. "You better believe I'm sneaking into your room tonight."

My face flushes as a nervous laugh bubbles up in my throat. "Cooper . . . My room is two doors down from our parents'. You cannot sneak in."

"The fuck I can't, Carys," he throws down the gauntlet, and my skin prickles with excitement.

"We'll see, Coop."

Not a single star shines in the dark and cloudy sky when we exit the Kingston jet in Philly. Cool air fills my lungs, and my fingers lace with Cooper's, hesitating.

His lips skim over my ear. "You okay, Carys?"

"Yes," I whisper on a shaky breath. Mom and Coach are waiting for us on the tarmac, and it suddenly all feels so real. So permanent.

Once we're at the bottom of the steps, Cooper's hand presses flat to my back and braces me as my mom runs over, crying.

She wraps her arms around me and holds me so tightly, I have a hard time breathing, until Coach steps in.

"Katie. Let her breathe." He has a thick arm around Cooper's shoulder, and when Mom finally releases me, he wraps me up in the kind of hug that makes you believe everything is going to be okay.

When we walk to the car, Cooper takes my hand in his again, and I watch my mother's eyes grow wide. She clears her throat and smiles a tentative smile. "Have you two kids worked everything out, then?" She nods toward our joined hands, and I fight the urge to laugh at her discomfort.

Instead, I tilt my head toward Cooper. "Have we worked everything out?"

He opens the car door for me and shakes his head. "Ya think?"

"Took you long enough to come around, son." Coach slides behind the wheel of his SUV, then looks at the two of us in the rearview mirror. "I warned you he was a little slow, Carys."

"Aww . . . I told Sabrina the same thing about Aiden."

Mom turns around to face us. "What happened to you boys in high school?" She laughs, and I bite down on my lip.

"Yeah, Coop. What *did* happen to you in high school?" I ask, equally loving this playful banter and feeling a little weirded out by it.

"Where's Callen?" It's closing in on eleven o'clock at night by the time we get back to the empty house and kick off our shoes.

"He's staying with Declan and Belles tonight. We'll grab him tomorrow. The Kings game is Sunday night, so we thought we could do a family dinner tomorrow or Thursday after practice." Mom brushes my hair away from my face, then gently cups my cheek.

I smile and kiss her palm. "Can we let you know, Mom? I think we're both still a little overwhelmed by everything and may need some time to decompress before you throw us into a family dinner."

She moves into the kitchen and makes us both a cup of tea while Coach and Coop stay in the other room to talk. Mom pushes a mug across the counter toward me, then passes me the honey and lemon. "So . . . how are you? Really?"

"I'm okay, Mom. My head hurts a little, but the doctor said that was to be expected. The stitches are dissolvable, so I don't have to have them removed. Don't get me wrong, I'm a little traumatized, but honestly, I'm more worried about Cooper than I am about me. He's acting like everything's fine. But it's not."

"Oh, honey." She sits next to me and holds her tea in both hands. "You might need to push him a little. Men like

Cooper like to be the one taking care of someone, not the one being taken care of. I'm not saying that's a good or bad thing. It just means he's going to need a little nudge to take care of himself." She sips her tea, watching me over the rim of her glass. "Everything between you is . . . ?"

I squeeze the contents of the little honey bear into my mug before looking up uncomfortably. We haven't talked about any of this since I stood in this kitchen and demanded to go to Germany. "It's good, Mom." I hesitate. "Is that weird for you?" I hold my breath and wait for her answer, knowing this could change my relationship with my mother permanently.

She wrinkles her nose. "A little. It's going to take some getting used to." She takes my hand in hers. "But honey, you never have to hide anything from me. Cooper Sinclair is a good man. And if you love each other, then Joe and I are happy, and damn anyone who isn't. You're bound to get a little media attention after yesterday though. So we should probably talk to Scarlet Kingston about that this week. Just so we can know what we'll be dealing with and how to handle it."

"No." I pull my hand away, not wanting any part of that for either of us.

My mom's eyes pop wide-open. "What do you mean *no*?"

"I'm not a celebrity, and I'm not an athlete on the Kings team. I don't need to talk to the owner, who happens to be a social-media specialist. I've never wanted that kind of spotlight, and I refuse to be forced into that now." I finish my tea and place the mug in the sink while I gather my thoughts. I know my mom is just doing what she thinks is right, but it's not what I want.

"I'll talk to Cooper about it, to see if he wants to meet with Scarlet, but it's a hard no for me. No media." I walk back over to her and kiss my mother's cheek. "I'm exhausted. I'm going to bed, Mom. I love you."

"I love you too, honey." She spins in her chair and gives me the *mom* glare. "Are you planning on sleeping alone?"

I glance down at the floor, wishing it could swallow me whole, just in the hope that I can avoid this conversation. "Umm . . . Do I have an option?" My voice squeaks as my cheeks flame.

"My door will be closed, dear. Unless you need me to check for monsters under the bed the way Callen does, I don't plan on leaving my room."

This may go down in history as the strangest conversation I've ever had with my mother.

But I think I just got permission to sleep with my boyfriend under her roof.

I'm going to take that as a win.

COOPER

"STOP POUTING, COOP," CARYS LAUGHS AS WE GET INTO HER car. The damn thing is the size of one of Callen's toys. *Christ*, my knees and nuts are practically smashed against my chest because I have to bend myself in half to fit inside.

"It's got eyelashes, Carys." She's got long black eyelashes on her pale-blue Volkswagen Beetle convertible. *Eyelashes*. "*Why* does the car have eyelashes?"

She puts the convertible top down, then jacks the heat all the way up. Turning out of Dad's neighborhood onto an old tree-lined street that leads us toward Kroydon Lake, she smiles like she just won an argument.

Like the top being down makes this better.

"The eyelashes are cute, Coop. And unless you have a car in town that I don't know about, this is our only form of transportation. So, hush." My girl blows right through a stop sign, and I groan.

"You know you're supposed to stop at those, right?" We did not just survive hell to die in a car with fucking eyelashes attached to the headlights.

"Cooper Sinclair." She turns toward me, and I slam my foot down against the floor, as if there's an imaginary brake that allows me to control the car.

"Holy shit, baby. How did I not know you're a terrible driver?" I soften the blow with a laugh, but given the silence during the rest of our ten-minute drive, and the stony glare she keeps shooting my way, I may have overshared.

We drive along the winding road, past the waterfalls and over to the side of the lake that's dotted with houses. Each one sits on a large plot with its own dock. Work trucks line the driveway of what I assume is Hudson Kingston's house. Daphne and he are talking near the driveway of a massive three-story home. Trees line the property, giving it privacy, and the lake sits off in the background.

I've been around money all my life. My father was a pro quarterback long before he started coaching, and my mother out-earned him every year as a supermodel. Money doesn't impress me. But this house is a whole other level of wealth.

Not that I should be surprised.

Hudson Kingston is a *Kingston*, as in the family who owns the Philadelphia Kings.

He's also the MMA heavyweight champion.

And he definitely seems like a *go big or go home* kinda guy, from the few times I've met him over the years. His sister is married to my buddy Bash, and Carys's best friend, Daphne, is engaged to his older brother, Max. Not to mention Dad and Declan coach and play for the Kings team. But he's a few years older than us, and we never ran in the same circles, so I don't know him well.

Carys gets out of the car and slams the door shut behind her. With a pissed-off fury on her face, she tosses me the keys. "You can drive home, since I'm such a terrible driver."

She tries to storm past me toward Daphne, but I grab her wrist and pull her back against me, taking her mouth in a kiss. "We all have to have flaws, baby."

She punches me in the stomach, and I laugh as Hudson

and Daphne join us. "Your form needs some work there, Carys." Hudson picks up her hand in his and moves her thumb to the outside of her fist. "Always on the outside, so you don't break your thumb."

Daphne pushes Hudson out of the way and throws her arms around Carys, and the two girls cry, while Hud and I stand there, watching like idiots.

"Nice house." I point behind us.

"Thanks. As big as my family is, we tend to end up with big houses." He looks behind him to see workers carrying in a piece of stone the size of a small room.

"We appreciate you letting us rent one of the others. Seems quiet back here, and we could definitely use a little quiet right now." Just thinking about the shitstorm of the past few months has my pulse pounding behind my eyes.

He leads me through the trees to the far side of his property. "Not a big deal. Honestly, it saves me some hassle. I had a realtor out here the other day. I bought the lot from a family who owned all three homes, but I only really wanted the one I'm remodeling. We were going over what needed to be done to sell the other two when Daphne called. The property hasn't even been subdivided into three separate lots yet. So you can take your time figuring out what you want to do. Rent or buy. Do whatever you want. If you change your mind, it's not a big deal. It gives me time to figure out my plan."

We stop in front of a two-story gray Cape Cod with stone and shaker siding. Dormers mix with rounded turrets and white trim. More trees line either side, so the privacy and views are similar to Hudson's place, but this one is less than half the size of his.

Thank fuck.

Hudson stands in a wide stance with his arms crossed. "So, what do you think?"

"Looks good to me," I tell him as the girls join us.

Carys wraps her arm around mine, a beautiful smile stretching across her face. Guess I'm forgiven for my comment about her driving. "Hud, this is perfect. Can we see inside?" Her entire body vibrates with excitement.

"Sure." He hands her the keys. "If you like it, you can move in today. I bought the place fully furnished. It's a little pretentious. Definitely something my mother would love. Lots of plaids." The last part is said with enough disdain that I think his mother and mine would probably get along. "Anything you don't want, just put in the garage. If you decide you want to stay for a while, we can get things moved out and put in storage. But you don't need to decide that yet."

Carys hugs him, and I fight back the growl clawing its way up my throat.

He's doing us a favor.

They're friends.

But he's touching my girl, and I fucking hate it.

"Good seeing you guys. Let me know if you need anything." He nods his goodbye and leaves.

"Alright. I have to get to work. Any chance you could get away for breakfast tomorrow morning, Carys? We could meet up with Chloe and Maddie at the Busy Bee." Daphne hugs Carys again, apparently not ready to let her go.

"Don't you have to work?" God, it's so fucking good to see her smile again.

"I'm sleeping with the boss. I think I can go in a little late. Max won't mind." She winks, and Carys laughs and checks out the huge engagement ring on Daphne's finger.

"Yeah, I guess you're safe." She kisses Daphne's cheek. "Breakfast should work. Thanks for everything, D."

"Anytime, C." Daphne kisses my cheek, and Carys shoves her gently.

Carys puts her hand on her hips and cocks her brow. "Hey, you've got your own. Leave mine alone."

I wait for Daphne to turn, then lift Carys from her feet and crush her to me.

Her legs wrap around my waist, and her arms circle my shoulders, clinging.

"Are you jealous, baby?" The thought sets my body on fire.

We walk through the front door. "Maybe a little. I mean, it's just Daphne. But still. I don't love seeing another woman's lips on you." She skims her mouth up my neck. "I'm the only person who gets to do that."

I set her on her feet, and she gasps and takes a step forward. "Oh, Coop . . . I love it." She turns back and takes my hand in hers, dragging me through each room. "This place is perfect."

"Yeah. It really is." High ceilings and an open floor plan combine with wall-to-ceiling single-pane glass doors that overlook a big backyard and the lake behind it. You can see Kroydon Falls further down in the distance, and huge hundred-year-old trees dot the shore as far as you can see.

She grabs my hand and pulls me upstairs, where four bedrooms and three bathrooms are spread out down a wide hall. The master takes up the entire far corner of the house, with a balcony the size of a small room overlooking the lake.

Carys places her palms against the railing and breathes in the cool fall air. "I love it."

I bracket her with my arms on either side of her body. "Good. Then let's take it. I didn't like sleeping without you last night."

"Sorry." She runs her tongue along her lips. "Though Mom didn't have a problem with it."

"Yeah well, Dad did. I figured it's best not to push it yet. I mean, Nattie and Brady lived together for four years, and I honestly think he believed they slept in separate rooms." *Denial* . . . it's not just a river in Egypt.

"Can we even afford it? I mean, I've got my trust, but did you and Hudson talk cost?" She worries her bottom lip, and I realize she and I have never had a conversation like this before.

I tug her away from the railing and sit down on the chair, pulling her onto my lap. "So, here's the thing. I knew I was never going to make the kind of money my parents made in the Navy, but I'm not going to lie and say I don't like having it."

Her eyes crinkle in confusion. "Alright . . . ?"

"I took a few online classes the summer after graduation and have added a few here and there when I could. I might not be Sebastian smart, but I'm really good at math. And I'm even better at the stock market. I've been investing since I was sixteen." I watch her carefully. "I've actually also been doing it for your brother, Declan, Brady, and Bash for the last few years."

Carys circles her arms around my neck and adjusts herself on my lap, confusion still evident in her eyes. "What are you saying, Coop?"

"I'm saying we can buy this house, if that's what you want. I'm saying I need to find a job because I could never be happy not having something to do. But if it takes years for me to find one, we'll still be fine. I can take my time figuring out what my next move is. Money isn't an issue, baby." I wait patiently while she processes what I just told her.

"So I guess you can afford to get a car without

eyelashes, can't you?" She giggles, then scoots off my lap and lowers to her knees. "The privacy here is incredible, isn't it?"

She pops the button on my jeans and slowly lowers my zipper, looking up at me through her dark lashes.

"Yeah." The word gets stuck in my throat as Carys drags down my jeans and boxers, and her delicate hands wrap around my hard cock.

"I don't give a single shit about the money, Coop. That never mattered to me." She circles her tongue around my balls as she tugs gently, and my eyes roll into the back of my head. "I just want you. I don't care where we live. I don't care what kind of house we have. I just need it to be with you." She licks the length of my dick with her hot tongue, and I forget everything we were talking about.

"I love the feel of your mouth on me, baby." I reach down and gently gather her hair away from her face, careful not to pull against her stitches, but needing to watch as the tip of her tongue plays with a pearl of precum leaking from the tip of my cock.

Jesus, she's fucking incredible.

Carys wraps her lips around the head of my dick and raises her eyes to mine as she takes me down into her throat. My abs contract, and my muscles tighten, and I think I could die just like this, watching her, and it would all be worth it.

A guttural, visceral groan leaves my throat as my head lolls back momentarily at the utter fucking perfection of this woman.

Carys hums as she picks up speed, jacking my cock as her velvety hot lips stretch, sliding up and down, and I shift my hips in sync with her.

"That's it, baby." Those eyelids flutter shut momentarily, and my thumb traces her jaw. "I wanna come right down your throat, Carys. Are you ready for me?"

She swallows me deeper and looks back up with tears in her eyes, gagging as her lips stretch tight around me. She nods at me as she picks up speed, wanting it as much as I do.

"Good girl, baby." I thrust deep into her mouth and come on a roar. "My fucking good girl."

COOPER

"THAT'S THE LAST BOX." MY BROTHER DECLAN SWUNG BY Dad's later today after practice to help me move anything worth taking from my old room and the few things Carys had left at Chloe's. Meanwhile, Carys and her band of merry women basically bleached the entire house while singing songs from *Grease* at the top of their lungs.

She emerges from the laundry room with a pile of sheets in her hands, laughing at something Maddie says. When they spot Declan and me, the laughter turns devious, and the two of them slide past us and up the stairs.

"What do you think that was about?" Declan catches one of his daughters when she dive-bombs him from a few stairs up.

"They're talking about boys, Daddy," Everly guilelessly tells him. "I heard Aunt Carys say Uncle Cooper likes—"

I swing Everly out of Declan's arms and cover her mouth. "Who wants to play helicopter?"

Declan rolls his eyes as Gracie runs into the room, yelling, "Me, me, me."

"Come on, munchkin." I lift her in my other arm. "Let's go outside."

"Cooper," Annabelle scolds with one hand digging into the small of her back and the other rubbing her very pregnant belly. "It's past bedtime, ladies, and we still need to pick up your little brother from Gigi and Grandpa's house."

I place both girls on the ground and watch them run for their little lives away from their parents. Annabelle presses a palm to my chest and straightens out my shirt. "It'll be really good to have you around for a while, Coop. We missed you."

I kiss the top of her head, and she places my hand over her stomach to feel a strong kick. "Definitely another little football player to add to the family."

She glares at Declan. "The last one."

"Yeah, babe. We'll see about that." He kisses his wife, then smacks her ass as she walks away. "Are you and Carys coming to the dinner at Dad's tomorrow night?"

"Yeah, I think so." Carys mentioned it yesterday, but we really hadn't talked about it yet.

"Well, try if you can. It'd be nice to try to do it more often, now that you're home." He claps my shoulder.

I never thought about that word as much as I have in the last few days. Home. I only lived full-time in Kroydon Hills for a little less than two years, but I guess this place really is home. "Yeah, man. I'll talk to Carys. Thanks again for the help today. I appreciate it." I pause for a moment before getting a little sappy with my brother. "And thanks for standing up for Carys when everything went to hell last month. She said Murphy and Nattie really railed against her, but you defended her. It means a lot to know you've always got my back."

"Always, Coop. But if you really want to thank me, take my kids for a night so I can have some time alone with my wife."

I shake my head, laughing. "I've faced down terrorists who are probably easier than dealing with your kids. You know that, right?"

"Yeah . . . well, they love you, so suck it up." He hugs me, then rounds Belle and the kids up to go home.

It's another hour before Maddie, Chloe, and Daphne have everything washed and put away the way Carys wants and finally clear out, leaving the two of us alone. The groceries have just been delivered, so I put them away, check that the doors are locked, then go search for Carys, only to find her curled up in a ball on the bed, asleep.

I pull a blanket over her and sit on the balcony with my phone in my hands, knowing I need to answer the text messages the guys have been sending for two days but not sure how.

Cooper: Hey fuckers. Carys and I are okay. We're back in Kroydon Hills. Pretty sure you all know that already.

Brady: Call your sister. She's driving me crazy.

Cooper: You can't return her now.

Brady: Dick.

Cooper: Ass

Murphy: Nobody's putting any dick in any ass in any sentence that could involve my sister.

Bash: Nobody but you, apparently.

Murphy: You guys staying with Mom and Coach?

Brady: They're not staying with Chloe. Nat and Chloe talked earlier.

Cooper: We spent last night at Dad's. Then moved into a house on the lake today. We're renting from Hudson Kingston.

Brady: Damn. That was fast.

Bash: We don't all marry our high school sweethearts, QB.

Brady: Yo Coop, when you get married, will your kids be siblings or cousins?

Cooper: Ha Ha Ha . . . very funny, shithead. Get it all out now.

Murphy: NO . . . No. No. No. Do not get anything out now. I don't want that thought in my brain.

Cooper: Not as much fun now that the shoe's on the other foot, is it, Murph?

Murphy: I'm gonna shove my shoe up your ass, Sinclair.

Bash: Let's get a drink this weekend, Coop.

Cooper: Sounds good.

Murphy: What about us?

Bash: You play for the enemy.

Cooper: You live in another state.

Brady: He just wants to hide from his pregnant wife. She wants too much sex.

Bash: WTF is wrong with you?

Murphy: Dude QB – you're a fucking traitor. Remind me to never tell you anything.

Bash: They've got pills for that, Murph.

Murphy: Whatever. I'm tired when I get home from practice.

Cooper: That sounds like a you problem, Murph.

Murphy: Says the guy in love with his sister.

Cooper: Yup. I have no problems with being too tired.

Murphy: Oh gross. Fucking stop.

Cooper: Happily. Night guys. I'm going to bed.

Brady: Hey Murph – he's going to bed with your sister.

Murphy: Assholes.

I shove my phone in the pocket of my pants and stare up at the stars, feeling lighter than I have in a long time.

"Cooper . . ." *Why is the ground shaking?* "Cooper, wake up."

My eyes open and flash around the room.

Where the fuck am I?

Carys presses a palm to my chest. "Hey. It was just a dream. I'm right here."

"Shit." I sit up and stare at her as I try to calm my rapid breathing and pounding heart. "Sorry. *Fuck.*"

I toss the blanket back and sit up, trying to pull my shit together, but it's not working.

The walls are closing in around me, so I jump out of bed, throw on my sweats and look around for a t-shirt. "I'm going for a run."

"You want some company? I need to meet the girls in a little while, but a run around the lake could be fun." She sits up on her knees and reaches for me, but I back up.

"That's okay. Why don't you go back to sleep for a bit? I'll see you when you get back from breakfast." I grab a pair of socks and my sneakers and kiss her forehead before leaving her alone in bed.

I need space.

A few minutes later, I'm pushing my muscles to the max as flashes of my dream dance in front of my eyes.

Her face with the gun against her head.

The sinister smile on Axel's face when he pulled the trigger.

The way she fell to the ground, but my feet couldn't move.

My body stuck in place.

Unable to get to her.

To breathe.

To react.

Her lifeless eyes.

I pump my arms harder and move my legs faster.

Trying to outrun the demons. But not sure if I can.

CARYS

The Busy Bee is one of the newer places along Main Street. They're only open until midafternoon, and the food is delicious. It's across the street from Hart & Soul, Annabelle's dance studio. A few other cute shops line the street too, but as I sit here with my friends, I find myself staring at the empty shop next to Sweet Temptations, the bakery Belle's best friend and Daphne's future sister-in-law, Amelia, owns.

The front windows are covered in paper, blocking my view of the inside. But there's something about it that's calling to me.

"Hellooo . . . ? Carys." Daphne throws a sugar packet at my head. "Are you even paying attention to me?"

"No, not really. Sorry." I met Daphne, Chloe, and Maddie this morning for breakfast, but my mind keeps going back to the haunted look in Cooper's blue eyes before he went for a run. Whatever dream he was lost in before I woke him up had to have been a nightmare. "I missed it. What did you say?"

The girls all shake their heads. "Nothing important. I'd say you've got the market cornered on the crazy life at the moment." Chloe steals the cherry from my plate of waffles, then ties the stem in a knot with her tongue and throws it at Maddie. "How was your date the other night, Mads?"

"Boring," Maddie pouts. "Not a single spark. I didn't even bother letting him walk me to my door. Of course, I doubt he even wanted to, considering Brandon was looking out the front freaking window, watching like a weirdo. I love my brother, but I don't know how much longer I can live with him."

"How was your first night in the lake house, Carys? Did you and Coop christen every room in the place?" Chloe elbows me as she wiggles her brows like a creepy cartoon character.

"No." I push my waffles around my plate, thinking about the way Cooper was thrashing in his sleep. "I think Coop's trying to avoid dealing with everything that happened. But he won't talk about it. And I'm worried."

"It's only been a few days. Give him time. My brother has never dealt with anything by talking about it." Maddie looks across the table with sad eyes. "I'm not saying that's the best way of dealing with things, just that he still may need time to process everything."

"Yeah. I guess you're right." Deciding I need a change of subject, I point across the street. "Do you guys know what's going in the empty shop next to Sweet Temptations?"

"Sam bought that shop." Daphne points further down the street. "And the two next to it. He wanted to make sure he had control over who moved in next to his wife. We all joked at the last family dinner that they should make the one right next door a day care they could put the kids in." She sips her orange juice, then coughs. "He didn't like that idea very much."

"Do you know if he wants to keep it empty?" My mind starts whirling with ideas.

Chloe shifts in the booth next to me. "What are you thinking, Carys Murphy?"

The waitress drops the check off at our table, and we each throw down a twenty, then scooch out of the booth. "I'm thinking, why don't we open our own boutique?"

Chloe pulls me behind her through the door of the Busy Bee. "There's no one in there, Chloe. Where are we going?"

Maddie and Daphne follow us through the door as Chloe leads us across the street. "We're going to talk to Amelia because you, my business partner, are a freaking genius."

I called Emerson on my way back to the lake house a few hours later to check in and tell her everything that was happening. Her mom is already driving her crazy, and she's ready to visit, just to get away after only forty-eight hours.

"You got this, Em." I pull into our driveway and see my mom and Callen standing by the front door. "Hey, Mom. What are you doing here?"

"Carys," Callen yells, then barrels toward me at full force.

I kneel down to brace myself for impact, just before little arms tackle me to the damp grass.

"Watch her head, Cal," Mom calls out to us.

"Carys, I missed you." He plants a sloppy, wet kiss on my cheek and squeezes me as tight as his chubby arms allow.

"I missed you too, bud. I didn't know you were coming over today." I look up at my mother, who's hovering with a reusable grocery bag in her hand.

Mom shrugs. "I was out getting some things for dinner tonight and picked up a few things for you. But we were just about to leave. I guess I should have checked to make sure you were home first."

"Cooper's not here?" I left three hours ago. He can't possibly still be running.

She shakes her head and hands me the bag as I stand up. "He didn't answer the door." Mom takes Callen's hand in hers and looks around the outside of the house, taking it in. "This is lovely, Carys. Do you think you guys will stay here long?"

I unlock the door and lead them into the kitchen. "I'm not really sure what we're doing yet, Mom. Cooper and I have to figure out a few things first."

"Is something wrong?" Mom asks as she empties the contents of the bag onto the counter.

I'm not sure how to answer her, but I have a weird feeling in my gut. "No. I don't think so. I just don't know where Coop is."

She finishes putting the containers in the fridge and hands Callen the empty bag. "Alright. Well, will we see you tonight?"

"Yup. We'll be there. What can I bring?" I hug her and then blow a raspberry against Callen's neck.

"Not a single thing. Just you and Cooper." She kisses my cheek. "Love you, honey." My mom holds my face in her hands for a moment, just looking at me, before she picks Callen up and carries him through the door.

I don't give myself time to overanalyze her behavior before I'm darting around the house, trying to find Cooper. When I get upstairs, I hear the water running and breathe a sigh of relief when I push through the bathroom door to find him standing under the shower.

Cooper washes the soap from his hair, then stares at me.

His vacant expression hurts my heart.

I toe off my sneakers, rip off my hoodie and jeans, and take special care with my bra and panties, placing them on the counter before stepping into the shower. Cooper is facing the water as it beats against him, and I massage his scalp while the soap suds wash away. I grab my loofah and add my body wash, then run it over his muscles. They're strung so tight, I expect them to snap under my touch.

And when I press my lips to the center of his back, Cooper does just that.

He turns and lifts me, slamming me back against the cool tile of the shower wall, yet still managing to cradle my head in his hand. "I need you, baby."

I kiss up his neck as my legs tighten around his waist. "Then take me, Coop. I'm yours. Take whatever you need."

My words give him what he wants, and he shifts us and thrusts into me on a grunt. Fucking me in a fury as the hot water pounds down on us. He buries his face in my neck and finds a hurried rhythm with his hips pistoning relentlessly, filling my pussy over and over.

Delicious waves of ecstasy pulse inside me as I claw at his back, moaning.

Cooper takes what he needs from me.

"You're mine. No one's ever going to take you away from me." His lips crash against mine. Violently.

Possessively.

"Never, Cooper. I'm yours. Forever." My legs shake as the first sharp jolt pulls me under, and I come on a visceral scream, pressing my mouth to his.

Giving him everything as he spills inside me silently.

We cling to each other, not moving for a few minutes before Cooper lifts his face. "Did I hurt you?"

I run my fingers through his wet hair. "No, Cooper. You saved me."

COOPER

"Are you sure we can't just stay home?" I ask, even though I know there's no chance we can. Skipping dinner tonight isn't an option, even if I'm trying to come up with a reason we can cancel as I grab a shirt from the closet.

Carys steps out of the bathroom in a pair of skintight dark jeans and a creamy sweater that falls off one shoulder, leaving her bare skin exposed. She smiles as she moves in front of me and buttons my shirt. Her hands skim my chest and spark a fire that never stops burning for her. "You look very handsome."

I grab her ass in both hands and squeeze. "I can think of so many things I'd rather spend the night doing to you, baby. Do we have to go?"

"Yes, we have to go. I owe Declan. If any of our family is going to go easy on us, it's Dec and Belles." She brushes a kiss to my jaw. "Don't pout."

"Men don't pout, babe," I tease, knowing full well I'm pouting. "We're stoic."

She drops a hand to my chest and trails it down along my abs. "How about this . . . ?" Carys sinks her teeth into her bottom lip. "If you come to dinner tonight, I'll let you do naughty things to me when we get home."

I grab her wrist and bring her fingertips to my mouth, kissing each one. "What kind of naughty things, baby?" My cock jumps in my pants at the words alone.

I wonder if the pharmacy has lube.

She leans in and whispers, "Anything you want."

"Let's go to dinner."

Family dinners are not a small thing in our family.

Nothing is small with as many of us as there are.

Carys parks her little clown car and takes my hand in hers. "You ready for this?"

"Do I have a choice?" I ask, only half serious—well, maybe three-quarters . . .

She shakes her head no and grabs the flowers we picked up from the market for her mom and hands me the bottle of wine. "Remind me why we're being so formal." I press my hand to the small of her back as we walk up the front steps of the house, knocking once before entering.

"Because I'm nervous, okay?" she admits with a slight tremble in her voice.

I place a chaste kiss on her lips, just as Gracie runs into the room and giggles, then yells, "Uncle Coop kissed Aunt Carys."

"And so it begins." Carys presses her forehead to mine. "Wanna make a run for it?"

"Nope. You said we had to be here. Now get ready because I hear more little feet." I press my lips to her forehead quickly, then catch Callen and Everly under my arms and fly them into the kitchen where Dad, Katherine, Belle, and Declan are waiting for us.

"Here." Declan hands me a beer after I put the kids down, and Annabelle deposits Nixon in Carys's arms.

"He's teething," Belle sighs and walks away.

"Uh, hi?" Carys looks around at everyone with wide eyes and a fussy baby.

Declan shakes his head. "That little devil was up all night last night and all day today. Which meant the girls were also up all night and all day. Belle's exhausted, the girls are hyper, and Nixon's pissed because Belle takes her boobs away every time he bites her." He hugs Carys, then adds, "Welcome to hell," and follows his wife out of the room.

Katherine finishes her glass of wine and pours another, filling it to the rim. "Welcome home, guys."

Nixon calmed down after they put him in a swing, and he chilled while we all ate dinner.

"Carys." Belle places her napkin on the table and smiles warmly. "I stopped by the bakery earlier and spoke to Amelia. She mentioned you and Chloe were taking a tour of the empty shop next to Sweet Temptations tomorrow. Are you guys thinking of opening a lingerie boutique?"

My head spins to Carys. "You didn't mention that earlier."

"Sorry," she whispers as a flush covers her face. "We were busy."

My brother laughs, and I kick him under the table like we're twelve-year-olds instead of grown men.

"That would be incredible, honey. Main Street has really had a nice revival over the past few years. I think you'd do well there." Katherine beams at the idea of Carys putting down roots in town, and I can see why. I just wish we'd had a chance to talk about it in private first.

"It really would–"

A loud bang rings out, and I throw myself at Carys,

taking both of us to the ground with my body covering hers. Shielding her. "Everybody get down," I yell.

Chairs scrape as the blood pounding in my ears intensifies.

"Cooper . . ." Carys braces my face. "Coop."

Fuck. My stomach drops as I realize no one else is moving.

"Look at me, Cooper." Her thumb traces my cheek. "Come back to me . . . We're safe, Coop."

"Cooper." Declan's hard voice demands my attention. "We're good. One of the girls pulled the microwave down, trying to get the cupcakes Belles put up there earlier. The girls are fine. Carys is fine."

Carys presses her lips to mine and whispers, "I'm safe, Coop. I need you to breathe for me."

I slowly look around as humiliation clutches me in its grips. "I'm so sorry." I move off her and help her up. "Are you okay? *Jesus*, did you hit your head?"

"I'm fine. Are you okay?" she whispers to me, while everyone stares intently at the two of us.

"Yeah, I'm fine. I think we should probably just go—"

"No," Declan and Dad say at the same time.

"Come on, little brother. Why don't you come outside with me?" Declan shoots me his *dad look*, and I feel like I'm about to walk the plank.

I look at Carys, who nods her head, encouraging me to go with him.

Declan and I walk into the backyard, the tension around us smothering me.

I move further away, not in the mood for him to act like some version of Dad with his *everything will be alright* speech.

"Listen, Dec—"

"No, Coop. *You* need to listen. You're not okay. You've

been dealt a shitty few months. And it just keeps piling on. But you've got to deal with it. Have you talked to anyone?" He stares at me, waiting. "Because when I asked Carys yesterday if you'd talked to her about any of it, she wouldn't say."

I don't say anything either.

Mostly because I don't know what *to* say.

"After Leah attacked Belles while she was pregnant with the twins, we went to therapy together for months." Declan sits down on one of the chairs surrounding the firepit and leans his elbows on his knees, a strangled expression etched on his face. "Want to know which one of us had the worst nightmares? Let me tell you, it wasn't my wife. The one held at knifepoint. It was me." He drags both hands down his face, reliving the worst day of his life. "The feeling that I failed her—that I caused it—haunted me. It still does."

"It was my fault, Dec. I can deal with what happened on the op. I don't like it, but I'm not responsible for it." I picture the look on Carys's face as she stared across her bedroom at me while Axel stood behind her. "She had a gun pressed to her head because of me." I drop into the chair across from him and hang my head. "I don't know how to deal with that."

"We're gonna deal with it together. Because that's what family does, little brother." I groan, and he ignores me. "Starting tomorrow. I'll be at your house at six a.m. Be dressed and ready to work out."

"What are we doing?" I push, wanting answers.

"Just be dressed and ready, Coop. Trust me." Declan kicks his feet up and gets comfortable.

I eye him skeptically. "Aren't we going back inside?"

"Nope. It's noisy as hell in there, and the girls just broke Dad's microwave. I'm staying right here where it's quiet.

So, since I'm staying right here. Might as well tell me what's been going on." The fucker smiles, thinking he's smooth.

But I tell him anyway.

All about the op.

About the hospital and finding out everything that went down.

The next few weeks in California.

The threats. The baby. Fixing things between Carys and me.

"Do you want to stay here in Kroydon Hills?" It's the first question he's asked since I started talking, and I don't have a solid answer.

"I don't know. I've got to figure out what the fuck I'm doing with my life, now that the Navy is done with me. I was looking into private contracting in California, but it sounds like Carys might want to stay here. We'll have to figure that shit out together." Guess it's time to start thinking about it. Probably past time. "I *also* need a car . . ."

COOPER

CARYS GIVES ME A REPRIEVE WHILE WE'RE AT DAD'S HOUSE. Once Declan and I move back inside, her worried eyes never leave me, but she doesn't push to talk until we're squeezed back into her car and she's given me the keys so I can drive home.

"Do you want to talk about it?" She takes my hand and holds it in her lap. "Or are you talked out after Declan? You guys were out there for a while."

Only a fucking saint would give me an out after that shit show earlier. "We were hiding from Dad."

"What did Dec have to say?" she asks quietly, her thumb rubbing soft circles over my palm. "Come on, Cooper. Talk to me. Don't make the mistakes I made. Don't shut me out."

I don't answer her.

Just keep my eyes on the road.

Not because I don't want to.

Because I don't know how to put it into words.

We ride the rest of the way home in silence.

The tension between us continues building with each mile, ratcheting up more and more as we get closer to the house. When we finally step through the door, Carys spins on me. "If you don't want to talk to me, you've got to talk to someone, Cooper. What happened tonight . . . I don't think that'll just go away."

I wrap an arm around her waist and tug her against me.

Wanting to feel her.

Needing it to ground me.

Carys rests her head on my heart and sighs.

That one little sound tells me we're okay. And it's a start. "I know I need to talk to someone. Declan wants me to go somewhere with him tomorrow. He's picking me up at six a.m. I promise I'll look into it after that."

"Where are you going that early? Doesn't Dec have practice?" She tips her head back, looking up at me as her fingers graze my jaw.

"He doesn't have to be at the stadium until later in the day." I search her eyes, looking for anger or hurt, but all I see there is love.

"You could always take my car," she offers, knowing there's no chance that's happening.

I bend down at the knees and throw her over my shoulder, spanking her ass. "That would be a *fuck no.* I need to buy a goddamned car that doesn't have eyelashes this weekend."

Carys pinches my ass as I carry her to bed.

"You gonna tell me where we're going?" Declan showed up at the house ten minutes early, but it didn't make a difference to me. I haven't slept in days anyway. It's still dark out, and the frost is already clinging to the grass outside.

I missed a lot of things about Kroydon Hills while I lived in California, but cold fucking winters were not one of them. I stuff my hands into the pockets of my sweats and climb into his old Bronco. "Dude, you're the highest-paid quarterback in the league. You want to maybe get a car from this century? This thing is older than both of us."

"Fuck off. I only take this old girl when I don't have the kids or Belles in the car with me."

When I snort, he punches my shoulder.

Fucking hard.

Asshole.

Declan turns the radio off as we head into town. "So, you know Scarlet Kingston married Cade St. James a few months ago, right?"

I nod. "Pretty sure somebody told me that. But please tell me we're not going to the football stadium. That's your thing, Dec, not mine." Not anymore.

His middle finger shoots up into the air. "Listen, you cocky little shit. It was yours for most of your life too. But no, we're not going to the stadium. We're going to Cade's gym, Crucible. He trains MMA fighters, including Hudson."

"I'm not against sparring." Running helped calm my mind yesterday. Sparring could definitely work.

"They also work with veterans. I thought it might be good for you. Meet some people. Hear some stories . . ." Dec trails off as we drive down Main Street, and I watch the storefronts pass by, wondering which one Carys and Chloe were looking at yesterday.

We pull up to the gym at six o'clock on the dot, and there's already a handful of cars parked there.

Guess we're not the only ones here.

I never came here as a teenager before I left for the Navy. But I'd heard of the place. Cade St. James was already a heavyweight champion by then, and Crucible was a big deal. When we walk inside, Hudson is warming up in the octagon with a guy who looks familiar.

What the fuck? "Dave?"

Dave's head swings my way, and Hudson knocks him

down, laughing, then spits out his mouthguard. "Thanks, Sinclair. I owe you one."

I step up to the octagon and hear a throat clear behind me.

When I turn around, Cade St. James stands behind me in sweats and a t-shirt, staring at my feet. "Shoes off the mat, Sinclair."

"Oh." I kick my shoes off and pick them up. "Sorry."

Cade shakes my hand. "Nice to officially meet you. My sister-in-law Lenny speaks very highly of you."

"Thanks. Lenny's great. Anybody who can deal with Bash is a saint."

Hudson laughs behind me as he and Dave climb down from the cage.

Cade eyes me. "Do you know anything about Crucible?"

"Not really. Only what Dec told me." I'm not sure what else there is to know, but it feels like I'm about to be tested.

"My dad is a retired marine, and this gym was his dream. His baby. He'll also be the first person to tell you it saved his life." Cade pulls his hoodie over his head and tosses it to the ground. "He had his own issues when he left the Marine Corps . . . I think a lot of us can relate to that."

Dave grunts. "I don't know if I'd have ever felt like myself again if it wasn't for this place. When I met you at that party all those years ago, Sinclair, I had life by the balls. An IED changed that. Changed everything. This place . . . this brotherhood. It helped me when nothing else could." He shakes his head with a smirk. "You know my sister actually works as a counselor for wounded vets now?"

"No shit? Tiffany's a counselor?" Jesus. I'd have never thought my ex-girlfriend would want to listen to anyone talk about their lives and their problems.

But I guess we all have to grow up eventually.

Cade opens the octagon door. "You've got to find a new mission. A new purpose. That's where people struggle. And that's where *we* can help. At least, until you figure out what you want to do."

Cade, Hudson, and Dave all stare at me for a minute like I'm a flight risk.

"Now, get in here and let's see what you got." Cade steps on to the octagon and bounces on his toes. "Hud, wrap his hands. I want to have some fun."

I'm about to step into the cage with a former heavyweight champion . . . Not sure *I'm* gonna call it fun.

Carys's car is in the driveway when Declan drops me off later, but I can't find her anywhere in the house. When I look outside, I see why. She's bundled under a blanket with her sketchbook in her hands and a white mug with a tea bag hanging out of it next to her.

She turns her head when she hears the door shut behind me, and a beautiful smile graces her lips.

There's nothing I wouldn't do to make her smile.

Nothing.

"Do I tell you enough how beautiful you are, baby?" I sit on the foot of the lounge chair and run my hands up her legs.

She leans over, pecking my lips. "You show me every day, Coop." She leans back and picks up her tea, then holds it in both hands, probably for the warmth. "How did today go? Where was this mysterious destination of Declan's?"

"A gym called Crucible."

"Oh, Cade's place. Maddie started teaching yoga there

last month." She stretches her legs across my lap and throws the blanket over both of us. "So, how was it?"

"It was good. I'm going back tomorrow." Her green eyes light up. "It felt good to be in that cage. The physical outlet . . . not having to think for a while. It helped. Hudson asked if I wanted to help with his training camp for his next fight." I was surprised by the offer but liked the idea.

"And? Will you?" She climbs into my lap and wraps the blanket around us.

"Yeah. For now. I told him I'd help until I found a job." Until I find a new purpose. "But it wasn't just that." I lean us both back against the chair and wait until Carys gets comfortable. "Cade's a retired marine. He's been through it and knows what it takes to get to the other side. And he has a program for vets. I actually knew one of the guys who was there this morning. He's a former SEAL. I dated his sister in high school."

"Tiffany?" Carys leans up, curious. "I remember her. What's she up to now?"

"She's a counselor who works with wounded vets." Carys huffs as she lays back down, and I smile. "Don't worry. I'm not calling her to talk about any of this shit. It would be a little too weird for me, but her brother, Dave, gave me the name and number of the counselor he talks to."

She presses her lips to my jaw. "Yeah?"

"I've got an appointment with her this afternoon." Not exactly looking forward to it, but I've got to start working on this stuff at some point.

"Coop, that's fantastic." Carys snuggles in closer, rubbing her body against mine. "Are you going to take my car?"

"No, baby. It's a virtual appointment. No need for my balls to hide inside my body because they're too embarrassed to be in your car." I wrap my hand around her throat and kiss her lips. "What did you do today?"

She wiggles in my lap. "I *want* to do more of that." She brushes her lips over mine, diving back in for more. Her soft lips nip my jaw as her hands slide into my hair. "Chloe stopped by earlier, and we went over numbers. I don't want to rush things, but when you're ready, we need to talk about where we think we want to stay. No pressure. But I don't know if you're thinking you want to stay here, or if you want to be back in California."

"Are you happy here, Carys? Is this where you want to be?" Her green eyes sparkle as her hair catches in the breeze, and I have the urge to freeze this moment forever.

"That's not fair. You can't answer a question with a question, Cooper. It's against the rules," she pouts.

"We already broke all the rules, baby." My fingers slip under her leggings and trace the dimples above her ass as I drag her closer. "I'm not tied to any specific place anymore. I like the idea of being here. Of being close to our obnoxiously annoying family. But what do you and Chloe want to do with the business? Do you want to stay here?"

"We still have more to talk about, but I think we'd like to stay here . . . at least for now. Chloe might want to expand into New York or California at some point, but if you and I want to stay here, we wouldn't have to move."

"Then let's stay here. I've been thinking about starting my own business, anyway. I can do that just as easily here as I could anywhere else." I stand up with her in my arms and walk into the house, only to find Hudson standing on the other side of the glass front door.

I sit Carys down on the kitchen counter and let Hudson in. "Hey, man. Everything okay?"

He holds up a case of beer and smiles. "I thought you

might want to watch some tape of my next opponent with me."

I look around him to see a car flying down the driveway and then turn back to Carys. "Looks like Bash is here too."

When Sebastian gets to the door, he bear-hugs me, lifting me completely off the ground. "Could you try to go more than a few weeks without almost dying, asshole?"

"Yeah. Let me see what I can do about that, dickhead. Aren't you supposed to be at practice? Declan was heading over an hour ago." The two of us join Hudson and Carys, who's already on the phone ordering pizza.

"Nope. I was there earlier. I'm done for the day." He turns and looks for Carys. "Mini-Murphy . . ." Bash waits for Carys to walk into his open arms. "How are you doin'?" He squeezes her waist with a devious glint in his eye, watching me.

"Back off, Beneventi. You've got a wife of your own."

"Eh, there's eight of us," Hudson scoffs. "Lenny's great at sharing."

Carys laughs at me, and for the first time in a long time, things feel a little bit lighter.

COOPER

One Month Later – Thanksgiving

"CAN YOU TIE THIS FOR ME?" CARYS WALKS INTO MY OFFICE on the first floor of the lake house and spins around in front of me. The black sweater she's wearing sets off her pale skin and scoops low in the back with no bra strap in sight. Instead, two lace ribbons hang down from her shoulders, waiting to be tied.

My girl loves her ribbons.

I stand from my chair and run my fingers down the soft skin of her spine, enjoying the goosebumps breaking out over her flesh. I press my lips to her bare skin as my dick jumps in my pants. "Baby . . . Do you want your brother to try to kick my ass during dinner?"

She tilts her head back and smiles. "*Can* my brother kick your ass, Coop?"

"Maybe in his dreams. But he's sure as hell going to try when he sees my eyes all over you today."

She huffs, then turns her head away from mine. "Tie the ribbon, Cooper. We're going to be late as it is."

My smile stretches, thinking about how Carys looked riding me earlier. We were playing with a very different kind of ribbon then. "Yeah, we are. But it was worth it." I

253

tie the ribbon on her sweater in a bow, and she turns in my arms and brushes her lips over mine.

"Totally worth it." She drags her teeth over my bottom lip, like a little tease, and smiles.

When she backs away, my eyes slowly drag up the knee-length black-leather skirt, hugging her curves, to the short black sweater that I know doesn't cover a bra. "So fucking sexy, Carys."

Her smile could light up the entire city. "So fucking yours, Cooper." Then she walks away, yelling, "Now get off the computer and let's go."

I've been working with Hudson's team for the past few weeks, and I love it. The physical outlet has been just what I needed, and being part of his team has definitely been an eye-opening experience.

But it's not enough. Yes, it's helped me work through the PTSD as much as my counselor has, but it's never going to be something I want to turn into a career.

I've been doing research on financial planning and investments. I was working on my business plan before Carys came in earlier. It may be a completely different direction than I originally planned for my life, but it works for Carys and me. And I like the idea of running my own business at some point.

Rook and I have talked about me potentially doing contractor work in some capacity for Phoenix. But Carys and I aren't ready for that right now, though we haven't ruled it out completely for the future.

I close the lid of my laptop and push my homework aside, then follow Carys to the kitchen. She's already pulled the appetizers out of the fridge. "Do we need to bring anything else?"

"Nope. Belles and Sabrina are bringing dessert, and Nattie and I were assigned appetizers." She grabs a bottle of wine from the counter and hands it to me. "And we're all bringing wine."

"*Great.* Because your brother getting drunk would definitely be a good thing today." She doesn't seem to pick up on my sarcasm as we step outside and climb into my new SUV without an eyelash in sight. "Is he making the turkey or is your mom?"

Carys shrugs. "I guess we'll find out."

It's complete chaos when we step into Dad's house. Everly and Gracie chase Callen, who's screaming while he runs away, holding a decapitated Barbie in one hand and swinging her head by the hair in the other. They fly by us, and I pull Carys back, so she isn't caught in their path of destruction.

Dad and Belles's brother, Tommy, are sitting on the couch in the family room, watching football on TV, so we stop and say hello before heading into the kitchen, where everyone else is crowded together.

Carys sets out our food and hands the wine over to Declan to open, while Katherine and Murphy argue over something in the oven.

"You're not twenty-one yet, Carys Murphy," Katherine scolds.

Carys quickly takes the glass of wine from Declan and scans the room. "Yeah, but I'm also not pregnant like the rest of them, so I think I earned one glass, Mom."

"Hey, guys." Nat turns to hug me, and her big belly blows my mind. From behind, my sister still looks like a normal-sized human. But from this angle . . .

"Nat, are you sure you don't have triplets in there?" I

lean in to kiss her cheek, not realizing what I said until she lunges for me.

Oops.

Brady grabs her by the waist and pulls her back. "No fistfights today, Natalie Grace. Your balance sucks. I don't need you going into labor two months early because your brother's a moron."

"Not a complete moron," Carys defends me. "But he sure is pretty to look at."

"Hey . . ." Yeah. I got nothing else. I'm lucky my sister didn't kill me.

Carys kisses Nat and Brady's cheeks, then tugs Nattie over to the table where Sabrina and Annabelle are sitting.

I move behind the island and stand next to Brady and Declan. "It's like an OB-Gyn office exploded in here."

"Dude, I don't know about Belles, but your sister is a fucking psychopath when she's pregnant. She can cry over a tissue commercial one minute and then be ready to throw a kitchen knife at me the next because I forgot to get her the right soy sauce. It's fucking scary." Brady smiles and waves at Nat across the room before she turns her pissed-off glare to me.

"So are you telling me I should hide the knives?" I really don't feel like getting stabbed today.

"Here." Declan hands Nixon over to me. "She won't stab you if you're holding Nix."

"He's a year and a half old. Doesn't he want to be with the other kids?" Brady plays peek-a-boo with my chubby nephew, just as Callen runs in and hides behind the counter.

He pulls on my pant leg. "If the twins come in here, you didn't see me."

I nod. "I gotcha, kid."

Brady slides over to block Callen from Everly's view.

"Okay, maybe don't let Nix play with the twins just yet . . . They're a little scary."

"How are Carys and Chloe doing with the shop? Will they be able to open on December first like they want? Chloe hasn't answered my calls all week, so I figure she's stressed." Brady moves to the side so Callen can dart away.

I glance over at Carys, feeling so proud of her. "Yeah. It got a little crazy there last week, but the shop's scheduled to open its doors in just under two weeks." They signed the lease for the building six weeks ago, and it's been full speed ahead since.

Murphy joins the three of us and passes us each a bottle of beer.

"What the fuck are you wearing, Murph?" I re-read his ridiculous apron. *Master Baster* is printed on his apron with a picture of a turkey in a roasting pan below it. "Dude. No."

"Come on. It's funny, and you know it." Murph looks over at the table full of girls. "Sabrina made me promise I'd stop with the innuendos before the kids are old enough to read, so I gotta get it in while I still can." He lifts his beer to his lips. "Just wait until you see next year's."

Carys moves next to me and kisses her brother's cheek before I watch her check in with her mom.

Damn. Her ass looks fantastic in that skirt.

A roll smacks me in the face. "What the fuck?" I glare at Murphy, who's laughing like an ass, with Brady and Declan trying to hide their faces.

Murph picks up another roll. "Stop looking at my sister's ass."

"In all fairness, she's *his* sister too." My eyes snap to Nattie, who just grabbed a piece of pepperoni bread from the island.

"You little traitor." I glare at my evil twin, but she shrugs her shoulders, then gives me the finger. "How about

257

you come up with another way to say I'm the size of a house, and we'll see what else I can come up with?"

One point, Nattie. She definitely won that round.

Dad steps into the kitchen and pulls two root beers from the fridge for Tommy and him. "What's got you guys laughing so hard over here?"

"Just busting Coop's balls, Coach." Murphy throws an arm around my shoulders, and Dad eyes it cautiously.

My gaze swings to Carys across the kitchen. "She's beautiful, asshole. And I'm allowed to look whenever I want."

"I'm not sure I'm ready to know, let alone see, what any of you are looking at," Dad teases.

Declan glances around the room. "More than half the women in here are pregnant, Dad. It might be a little late for that."

Dad takes the beer out of Declan's hand, takes a sip, then hands it back. "There's knowing, and there's seeing for yourself. Two very different things, son."

Murphy sprays the beer in his mouth out through his nose as he chokes. "Yeah, Coach. Pretty sure I found that out the hard way."

The rest of us laugh. "Yeah, Dad. That kitchen table looks new. Doesn't it, Murph?" I goad him. The tales of Murphy walking in on Dad and Katherine having sex on the table will never get old.

"It actually is, Cooper." Dad leans in close and drops his voice. "Because the old one wasn't sturdy enough to do what I wanted to with your girlfriend's mother."

He takes my beer bottle and taps it to the top of Murphy's so the foam rises and spills over the sides.

Dad walks away while Brady absolutely loses his shit because he's laughing so hard. "And that, my friends, is a mic drop moment."

I tap Murphy's shoulder, after the dinner dishes are done, and motion for him to follow me outside.

His shoulders deflate, like a kid about to get yelled at. "Come on, Coop. You can't be pissed. It was a funny joke."

I keep walking until we're far enough away from the house, then turn around to face him. "I didn't even hear the joke, Murph. I brought you out here to tell you I'm going to ask your sister to marry me."

One side of Murph's mouth pulls up in a shit-eating grin. "Is this you asking for permission?"

"No, asshole. I asked your mom for permission. I'm *telling* you out of respect. But don't say anything to anyone else yet. I want to make sure it's a surprise." I pull the box out of my pocket and show him the ring I bought weeks ago.

He whistles long and low. "Damn, man. That's beautiful."

"Thanks. I hope she likes it." I stuff it back in my pocket and ignore the goofy grin growing on his face.

"Do you know when you're gonna pop the question?" I shake my head, and he holds his bottle of beer up, waiting for me to do the same. "To my favorite sister marrying my favorite brother." He taps his bottle to mine, and I shake my head.

"You really are an asshole," I laugh.

"Yeah well, are you gonna be my brother-in-law or my stepbrother?"

I ignore his stupid jokes. "I'm going to be the man who loves your sister every day for the rest of her life."

"Good answer, Cooper. Good answer."

I sit in our bed later that night with the ring in my hand, still unsure of when I want to ask her. I thought it might be easier after I talked to Murphy, but it's not.

I've put so much thought into the how and when, but nothing's seemed right . . . until now.

The door of the bathroom cracks open, so I shove the box back into my nightstand drawer and watch as Carys steps out.

She takes my breath away, walking toward me in lacy-blue lingerie and spinning in a circle. "Do you like it?"

I don't answer her because the words are stuck in my throat. She walks across the room and climbs up on the bed. "Hey, you feeling okay, Coop?"

I lift her onto my lap and gather her face in my hands. "You are the love of my life, Carys Murphy. The air I breathe. I've tried to figure out how to do this about a million times over the past few weeks, but nothing seemed right."

She tilts her head and wraps her fingers around my wrists. "What are you talking about, Cooper?"

"We've done everything differently from the very beginning. It's always just been us. We didn't need anyone else, so I wanted to do this in private. Just you and me." I wrap an arm around her waist and kiss her softly. "Sixty years from now, when we're old and gray, sitting outside on this lake, I want to look back and know I've lived a good life. A worthy life. I want to be a good man who's worthy of you. And if I only do one thing right in this life, I want you to know that I love you completely. Fiercely. No holding back. With no regrets." I reach inside the night-stand, pull out my feather, and hand it to her.

"The feather?" She runs her finger softly over the vane and smiles a sad smile. "I'm not sure it was exactly the good-luck charm I hoped it would be." She spins it in her hand, then looks back up at me.

I lift the diamond ring from my drawer and slip it on her finger. "I don't think it was the feather, baby. I think *you* were the good luck. I held on to that feather because you gave it to me, but you were what I was holding on to. What I was coming back for. And when I didn't know if I was ready for all this, you stayed by my side until I opened my eyes to what was right in front of me."

A single tear falls down her cheek.

"Marry me, baby. Walk by my side for the rest of our lives. No matter what that looks like. The good, the bad, the crazy highs, and the awful lows. Marry me, so we can take care of each other forever." I lift her hand to my lips and kiss her fingers.

She nods her head as more tears spill freely. "Of course, I'll marry you, Cooper Sinclair. I love you."

"More than the air I breathe, Carys."

CARYS

EPILOGUE

I FLIP THE SIGN ON THE DOOR OF LE DÉSIR TO *CLOSED* AND hurry next door to Sweet Temptations, where I'm meeting the girls for coffee. The shop officially opened the first week in December, and it's hard to believe how busy we've been in the five months since. Chloe's already negotiating new contracts with a manufacturer and a new supplier in California, so we can keep up with demand.

We've been trying to get together once a week since football season ended a few months ago, when Aiden and Sabrina and Nattie and Brady all moved back to Kroydon Hills for the off-season. Well, we also waited a month or two because . . . so many babies.

I swear, the girls gave birth like dominos.

Belles started it off in December, having a beautiful little boy, who they named Leo.

Sabrina was next, with my nephew, Jameson.

Nattie followed, managing to make it to thirty-seven weeks before Lyla and Noah joined the family.

Lenny and Bash's son, Maverick, was the last little one to be born, making his entrance a month after the twins.

I basically get to snuggle a baby whenever I want, then can give them back to their parents when they get cranky or blow out their diaper. Definitely my version of winning.

During football season, it was only Chloe, Daphne,

Maddie, and me who would meet here or at the Busy Bee. But once the other girls came home, our little foursome grew. And apparently, I'm the last one to arrive today. I wave, make my way to the counter for a Chai tea and vanilla-bean cupcake, and then join our crowd in the back corner. I steal Jameson from Sabrina and sit down. "What's up, ladies?"

"Shouldn't we be asking you that?" Nattie cuddles a sleeping Noah while Chloe holds a bottle to Lyla's lips. "Are you ready for this weekend?"

I glance over at Chloe. "We're doing my final fitting this afternoon. And most of our friends from California are flying in tonight or tomorrow. Mom's got the caterers and florist handled, and I spoke to Jack this morning. He promised they'd be here Friday morning."

"I still can't believe Six Day War is playing at your wedding, Carys. I love them," Belles informs me for the millionth time since Jack and Theo confirmed they'd be able to be here for the wedding.

Daphne swipes her finger through my frosting. "I guess it helps when you have a writing credit on their first hit song."

"I guess." I blush. "They'll always just be Jack and Theo to me."

"Lucky bitch," Belles snickers.

"Says the girl married to the number-one quarterback in the country," Nattie chides.

Lenny shakes her head. "You're just salty that Brady is ranked seventh. I already reviewed his stats with him and told him how to improve them."

"Your brain scares me, Len," Sabrina says softly.

Lenny laughs. "The Secret Service agents around the room don't make you feel safe enough, Sabrina?"

Maddie leans over and whispers in my ear, "The one

over there is kinda hot. Are they allowed to date her friends?"

We both giggle. Jameson's big green eyes pop wide open, and he gazes up at me and smiles.

We spend the next hour talking about anything and everything I might still need to do for Saturday. All the girls act like I should be stressed about it all, but I'm not. I don't really care about most of it. I love my dress. Chloe and I designed it ourselves. I love the dresses Chloe, Daphne, Maddie, and Emerson will be wearing too. We've got an enormous tent rented for the backyard at our house, in case it rains like it's supposed to, but even that doesn't worry me. Cooper and I had some of our most intense moments in the rain.

Some good, and others not so much. But they've all led us here.

Chloe and I don't stay too long today before we head back to Le Désir and finish my final fitting. My gown is a beautiful white French crepe that drapes perfectly, skimming my body and hugging my curves. The bodice dips into a low V in the front and is held in place by thin straps that wrap around each shoulder and show off my entire back, dropping into a dramatic cowl right above the dimples at the base of my spine. Tiny white buttons start there and make my ass look fantastic as they form a line down to the train.

It's incredibly simple and incredibly perfect for me. I love it.

Better yet . . . I think it'll drive Cooper wild when he sees me in it.

COOPER

Declan and I stand at the end of the aisle, in front of the dock on our property, which we bought from Hudson a month ago. We're waiting for the girls to make their way down to us, but they still haven't appeared. Carys has four bridesmaids and Everly and Gracie as flower girls.

I didn't want to have enough groomsmen to form a football team, so I asked Declan to be my best man and left it at that. Murphy is walking Carys down the aisle, and Brady and Bash, along with Ford and Trick, are all helping me out as ushers. Rook stands behind Declan and me, ready to officiate our ceremony.

Ford's still in the Navy, working as a trainer in Coronado. Rook finished up his time and left for private contracting with his brother's company. Trick was medically discharged, along with Wanda, who never served again after our last op. Now, she's a very happy, spoiled pet, who's sitting at the end of the aisle, next to her human. We all came away from that op with our own demons, and Wanda helps Trick deal with his.

The music changes, and the bridesmaids finally line up at the back of the aisle.

"You ready for this, Coop?" Declan smiles proudly at me as Emerson begins her walk down the aisle, followed by Maddie, then Daphne. Chloe turns around and says something to Everly and Gracie before she, too, walks toward us.

The twins wear matching white dresses with emerald-green ribbons tied around their waists. They scatter red rose petals along the aisle runner as they skip toward their father. I'd love to say I notice anything else, but I don't. Because that's when Carys and Murphy step up to the end of the aisle and wait.

She is magnificent.

Her hair is pulled back in some kind of intricate, low bun at the nape of her neck. Her dress is simple. No rhinestones or sparkles. Just a gorgeous dress draped over her beautiful body. The only flashy thing about her are the emerald earrings I bought her for Christmas and the smile stretching across her face as she walks to me.

When she reaches the end of the aisle, Murphy takes her hand and places it in mine, then kisses Carys on the cheek. "Love you, Care Bear."

Her smile stretches wider. "I love you too, Aiden James." Then she turns to me, places her other hand in mine, and winks. "What do ya think, Coop? Still want to marry me?"

"More than my next breath, baby."

The End

WHAT COMES NEXT

WANT TO SEE MORE OF COOPER AND CARYS'S WEDDING? Enjoy this bonus epilogue!

Download here!

Not ready to say goodbye to Kroydon Hills just yet? Don't fret. Follow the Kingston family as they each figure out what comes next while falling in love in the new series, Defiant Kings.

Hudson Kingston's book, Caged, is available for preorder. Pre-order Caged

ACKNOWLEDGMENTS

M ~ Thank you for everything you took on so that I could write this book. Without you, none of this is possible.

To my very own Coop ~ We pulled it off! I was getting kind of worried there for a minute.

My editor, Dena. Without you and your dedication, I'm not sure that I ever would have typed "The End".

Hannah ~ When we started talking about a shared world I had no idea how excited I would be to write those characters. Thank you so much for lending me Rook!

Heather ~ You have been the most amazing addition to our team. Disney here we come.

Vicki ~ I think I may actually have time to fill my cup now.

Sarah ~ Thank you so much for putting up with me.

To my Betas ~ Nichole, Hannah, Meagan, Shawna & Heather. Thank you for helping me make Coop & Carys everything they deserved to be. I appreciate each and every one of you!

My Street Team, Kelly, Shawna, Vicki, Ashley, Heather, Oriana, Shannon, Nichole, Nicole, Hannah, Meghan, Amy,

Christy, Adanna, Jennifer, Lissete, Poppy, Jacqueline, Laura, Kathleen, Diane, Jenna, Keeza, Carissa, Kat, Kira, Kristina, Terri, Javelyn, Morgan, Victoria, Jackie, Andrea, Marni ~ Thank you, ladies, for loving these characters and this world. Our group is my safe place, and I'm so thankful for every one of you in it. Family Meetings Rock!

Shannon ~ you are so talented! Thank you for bringing these covers to life.

To all of the Indie authors out there who have helped me along the way – you are amazing! This community is so incredibly supportive, and I am so lucky to be a part of it!

Thank you to all of the bloggers who took the time to read, review, and promote Ending The Game.

And finally, the biggest thank you to you, the reader. I hope you enjoyed reading Cooper & Carys as much as I loved being lost in their world.

ALSO BY BELLA MATTHEWS

Kings of Kroydon Hills

All In

More Than A Game

Always Earned, Never Given

Under Pressure

Restless Kings

Rise of the King

Broken King

Fallen King

The Risks We Take Duet

Worth the Fight

Worth the Risk

The Defiant Kings

Caged